Lanterns In The Mist

Also by Edward Fotheringill

Darkness Withdrawn OR The Eclipse of Nietzsche's Shadow

Lanterns In The Mist

Edward Fotheringill

Booklocker.com, Inc.
2007

In Memory of Edward Leon Fotheringill (1919-2004)

Dreams. Dreams in the unfolding, fertile awareness of the human race. Flickering images, never completely transparent, appearing and disappearing across the screen of human consciousness. Dreams breathe through the pulse of a subjective, inner landscape which is, at the same time, paradoxically personal and collective. Some dreams flash out during the waking state. They pick us up and compel us toward our destiny. Some dreams germinate out of the sleeping state. They reveal fragments of meaning, fragments of our possibilities. They are the threads with which myths are woven.

Then, there is The Dream. The Dream in the Mind of God. This Dream has no boundaries, personal or universal. It includes everything because it includes no-thing. Everything possible in the waking state is there. Everything possible in the sleeping state is there. This Dream displays no fragments, only the totality of pure possibility. This Dream harbors all myths before their time.

1

Bali-1981

Beneath the weight of dark morning shadows, he lies on a bare mattress in a thatched-roof hut. He is thin and weak with fever. His face is drawn and sallow behind a bushy beard. The sleep in which he is immersed is not peaceful. It is the kind of sleep we enter with dread. For we know what's coming. We've been there before.

Eyelids dancing a distressed jig. A grimace plants its dark roots around his mouth. Now a deep, guttural sound coming from his belly. His mouth opens fitfully. The sound is pitching higher. A wailing comes up through his torso causing chest, throat, and lips to convulse. With a shuddering start, he awakens. Breathing heavily. Perspiring. Weeping. The very marrow of his bones aches. It is another day.

The dreamer has relived, for too many nights now, a crushing horror of the waking state. In the mountain village of Bayung Gede, where goiter is common due to generations of thyroid deficiency, a twelve-year-old girl has turned into something unspeakable. What is thought to be a baseball-sized goiter at the base of her throat is the least of her problems. Her once beautiful copper-lustered skin is now the color of black ash. Her coal black hair has turned gray. Her aqua-green eyes are now incandescent yellow. Her tongue is blood red and entertains foul, gray spittle. She speaks in tongues, and on occasion, porcine whines and howls emanate from deep in her belly. Unfathomable evil lurks here.

He enters the mud hut armed with Bible and holy water. It is the seventeenth day he has done so. He is collapsing from exhaustion. The hut reeks of vomit and excrement. Two elders of the family, both women, are attempting to sponge bathe the child. Not long ago the girl was playful and happy, singing nursery rhymes and dancing to

9

the gamelan drums of village musicians. Now she is in no man's land.

He asks the elders to step aside. They huddle in a corner of the hut. They brace themselves, as they have done sixteen times before, for what's to come. The priest decants some holy water from a Coke bottle into the palm of his hand. With this provocation the child slithers like a snake across the floor. The priest stalks her and flicks the holy water on her head. As the water makes contact with her forehead, black puffs of soot-smoke evaporate into the air. The child shrieks as burn marks appear on her brow. The goiter at her throat expands like a balloon at the lips of an excited child celebrating a birthday.

*Now the girl resembles nothing human. It moves along the ground like a spider in distress. The priest is chanting adamantly: **"By the power of Christ, I command thee...By the power of Christ, I command thee..."** Like an anticipatory cat with back arched, the thing is skittering across the floor, sideways. It stops suddenly. Hissing. Yellow eyes darting back and forth.*

"Our Father, who art in heaven..."

*The thing slowly turns its head. It has the elders in mind. The old women huddle in a corner of the hut, faces turned away, sobbing. **"...Thy kingdom come, thy will be done..."** They never see what hits them.*

*In an astonishing display of brutal athleticism, the thing pounces with the force of a hurricane. Arms flaying, legs kicking, thin calcium poles covered with skin execute the bloodletting. In a matter of moments, two battered, faceless heaps lie in the corner. The thing, covered with blood, is giggling. Belching. The smell is foul. Its tongue darts around its lips, looking for and finding blood and skin fragments. It speaks. **"Your turn, Padre."***

The priest has had enough. The Bible drops to the floor. He involuntarily raises the Coke bottle to his lips and drinks deeply of the holy water. Is it blood he tastes? A cold shadow of transcendent energy steals over his eyes like cataracts. His breathing is deep, slow, powerful. The thing is moving once again. Slithering across the dirt floor of the hut. The priest stalks it. His eyes do not blink. A fixed, relentless stare. He has it cornered.

Nothing purely human exists in this forsaken hut in the mountains of Bali. Two forces of nature. Two poles of concentrated energy. No conscience to redirect the forces. The priest leaps like some forgotten feline ancestor. He has the creature by the throat. Pinned to the dirt floor. **"By the power of Christ, I command thee..."** *The thing jams its fingers—they are like claws of molten steel—into the ribcage of the God-man on top of it.* **"By the power of Christ, I command thee..."** *The pain is unbearable, radiating up through his torso and down through his thighs. His grip on the thing's throat tightens like a vise. The eyes of the thing are turning red. Is it blood he sees? A faint numbness saturates his body.* **"God above commands thee...God above commands thee...LEAVE THIS CHILD OF GOD!"**

The priest is gone now. Numb as death. Floating above it all, he witnesses the struggle beneath him. The thing's eyes are flashing. Red—green—red—green. Green. Aqua-green. The little girl screams a piercing cry signaling a fresh awareness of the present. Black bile gushes from her mouth. With each expulsion the swelling in her throat mercifully deflates.

Bali. The mountain village of Bayung Gede. A mud hut. Darkness. Stillness. Two shadowy heaps lie in a corner like discarded bundles of hay. A child is crying. Here we have human tears. A body lies on top of her. A heavy weight with no will of its own.

11

2

One Year Later

For two years now the Goa Gajah Temple had been his home. An incongruous fact, especially for a Catholic priest. Twelve hundred years ago the temple was constructed and occupied by Buddhist monks. In the still hours of the morning, if one is quiet enough, faint echoes of *OM MANI PADME HUM* can be heard in the wind. Since the eleventh century, Goa Gajah has been the home of Hindu monks. Bali is this way: it is a place where the force of underlying unity prevails.

From his thatched-roof hut on the hillside, he could see the temple courtyard above him and the deep jungle river valley below. The rarefied air of open space and silence allowed his life of discipline and solitude to take the form of simplicity itself. Long hours in meditation, solitary walks along the river's edge, sleeping little, eating less. A monk removed from the conventional paths walked by ordinary men and women.

He had spoken little in the past year—in fact, only when the exigencies of life made it absolutely necessary. The self-imposed vow of silence was precipitated by a horrific seventeen-day exorcism leaving him temporarily paralyzed from the neck down. Upon recovery, silence became the curative tonic in which he bathed. The stillness had drawn him inward—to a point where the recesses of his inner life opened up to a vastness only the mystics really know.

This morning an intuitive awareness told him it was time to return to the world. This was why he had come to Bali: to prepare himself to go back to the world. Those who really want to give themselves to humanity must first abandon the world—and may authentically return only after emptying themselves completely of selfishness, fear, and expectation. For him, there would be no more demands on life. Rather, he would be a still and empty vessel waiting to be called by life's curious happenings and interplays to serve humanity (in ways he would never imagine). In later years he would say, "I am a puppet. The movements of life pull my strings."

This morning he put on sarong, sash, and headdress and rode his bicycle to Monkey Forest Street in Ubud where he marched in a grand funeral procession for an old Brahmin priest. In the clearing of the forest where the cremation was held, he felt some previously imperceptible tension in his chest and forehead *snap* just as the great white ceremonial bull housing the Brahmin's body went up in a white-hot blaze. Standing fast and close to the raging inferno, he felt all sense of finite self melt away. What was left of him merged lightly with the fire's palpable heat.

When the burning body of the Brahmin collapsed through the gutted belly of the white bull and fell to the charred, corrugated-metal sheet resting on the platform below, the flaming head separated from the body with an eerie *pop*, rolled off the metal sheet, and came to rest at Father Byron's feet. Blue, dagger-like flames shot through the sockets of eyes and mouth and bled orange at the blackened skin. The charred, eyeless skull stared him down with a look that spoke of eternity.

Twenty-four hours later, somewhere over the Pacific, Father Byron stared into the lavatory mirror of the Boeing 747. He did not recognize the face staring back.

3

Baltimore-1993

The Robert E. Lee Memorial Park. A glorious fall day beckons the night with sunset. Golden orange light floats on the treetops and crystallizes in the crisp fall air. A pack of wild dogs, in silhouette, moves in unison across the horizon, the bloodline of wolves palpitating in every cell. With a collective sweep of their mangy heads, they find an agreeable scent and change direction as if being pulled by a magnet.

When she woke, the dogs were all around her—sniffing her hair and nudging her arms and legs with their muzzles. Clenching her fingers into fists, she moved her arms in front of her face and raised herself to a sitting position. With prescient pause, she sat still as a statue. The dogs explored her—moving in a tight circle like one coordinated organism. Tilting forward, balancing herself on the balls of her feet, she thrust herself upward to a standing position. There must have been ten dogs. Mutts. Street dogs. Silver, black, gray, brown. Dull, matted fur. Breathing heavily. Some stayed at her feet, pushing their muzzles against her calves and ankles and the tops of her shoes. Others quietly dispersed. After some time she walked slowly toward the bridge leading out of the park. She kept her head up—her eyes fixed on the bridge in the distance. She felt the dogs drop away, one by one. Until there was only one. This one, big and bulky and thick with coarse hair standing on end, hovered with her, breathing heavily, as she moved.

An insidious, guttural growl vibrated beneath her. She stopped. Looked down. Looked directly into the eyes of that incongruous beast. This creature was more like a wolf than a dog—a wild thing not to be trusted. It glared at her with red eyes, teeth bared, nostrils flared. She stared, without fear, into the depths of those red eyes—

daring fate to take its course.

For a moment, she felt invisible. That she wasn't there at all. Then, as if in a metaphysical wind tunnel, she heard the creature speak: *Oh, my sweetie. If only you knew how easy it would be to rip you limb-from-limb.* The creature spoke in a husky groan that issued forth out of the darkness of another world. *If only you knew how quickly I could render you useless and drain the sweet lifeblood from your body into mine. Are you ready, my sweetie? Are you ready to die? I can taste your warm blood already. Your fear makes it warm.*

An uncanny stillness spread out within her. Cold and steely and impenetrable. Then she heard a voice issuing forth from somewhere deep inside her. The voice and its origin unrecognizable. *You want to kill me, little dog? Is that what you want? Fine! I'll be your dinner— but know this: my blood will course through your veins like sharp shards of icy glass. You may be evil, but you're not wise. You've selected for your prey someone who's already dead. I really don't care what you do to me!*

The invisible turned visible again. The animal growled and scraped the ground pensively with its sharp claws. Its red eyes ominously darted back and forth. Then, inexplicably, it began to whimper. It turned its head away and lumbered off.

The cool fall air caressed her face like a gentle lover. The orange sun gleamed through the tree line like some suspended ornament of grace. Open spaces of silence hovered between the chirring of crickets. Then, in a movement of spontaneous gravity, she felt her body pulled to the earth. She sat in the leaves and wept. The tears were a great release, a sign of deep cleansing. After some time, she smiled and understood.

4

She sat in her car in the country darkness of Corbett Road beneath an old, cock-eyed lamppost. The light gave off a metallic glare that spoke of interrogations given up long ago. Surprisingly, she felt exceptionally calm. *He's not an ordinary priest,* she thought. *I've got to remember that.* She stoically laughed at herself. *So this is what it's all come to.* At her turn of the key in the ignition, the Volvo came to life. Winding her way through the wooded stretch of serpentine road, she felt destiny's hand pushing her along.

Navigating the last turn of the uphill driveway, she could see a mystical, yellow glow through the gray-black skeleton of low-lying thicket. *The proverbial light at the end of the tunnel,* she thought wistfully.

The wind swirled gently in the darkness, and a cool mist danced on the bare splinters of yellow light cast from the windows of the priest's house. Nestled in the hills of Monkton, Maryland, the compact, white stucco bungalow radiated the cool stillness and solitude of a hermitage.

A hooded figure sat on his haunches against the side of the house, enveloped in the damp evening darkness. Only a cigar's dull orange glow illuminating the relaxed hands of the shrouded shape gave any hint of human presence to the woman approaching the house.

As she walked, she was engulfed by some temporal slowdown. She witnessed her movements in slow motion and knew, uncannily, that all of it had been decided long before. Hearing her own voice, she was brought back to the present moment: "Excuse me. I'm looking for Father Byron."

Out of the emptiness of the moment, the hooded figure nodded, rubbed out the cigar in the damp soil, and got up. "I'm Father Byron."

"I'm Lisa Browning." The tall, meaty, middle-aged woman caught sight of her shadow projected across the misty lawn. *Is that the way life is?* she thought. *Like an effervescent shadow? Here one moment, gone the next?* "I have an appointment with you."

"Yes, I remember." The priest looked at his watch. "You're right on time."

Lisa smiled. "Punctuality is one of my many virtues."

The priest laughed. "Is humility another of your *many* virtues?"

Lisa Browning stood frozen in silence. She sensed this encounter would be unnerving. It didn't help that the countenance of the priest was barely visible beneath the black, hooded parka. It was as if she were talking to a ghost. "I guess not," Lisa said, shaking her head in embarrassment. "Well, it's always nice to make a good first impression."

The priest smiled. "You're doing fine." Projecting his gaze to the muddy ground before him, he swept his feet across the soil as if he were a baseball player preparing the batter's box before digging in to hit. "I must ask you: how did you find me?"

"I got your phone number from Father Welch at St. Mary's Seminary."

"Ah, Father Welch." The priest playfully rocked back and forth on his heels. "Did he tell you I don't receive many visitors?"

Lisa turned slightly to shield her face against a gust of wind. "I was told you would make yourself available to those who could find you."

"Well, you seem to have found me," the priest said, sighing. The words hung heavily in the evening mist. "Why me? Why have you come to me?"

"I have my reasons," Lisa said convincingly. "I heard about you several years ago from a mutual friend. I think you'll remember him."

The priest cocked his head quizzically. "Don't keep me in suspense."

Lisa's eyes twinkled playfully. "Ronald Maris. You helped him with a rather delicate problem."

The priest was silent. Darkness stretching into infinity under the hood of the parka. "Ah, yes. Ron. I was glad to help."

Lisa flushed with embarrassment. "Please don't think Ron was broadcasting this event indiscriminately," Lisa said, suddenly worried she had given a wrong impression. "As far as I know, I'm the only person he ever confided in." Lisa gently touched the priest on his forearm. "Ron thinks the world of you. He literally owes you his life."

The priest held up his hand like a traffic cop preparing to make safe passage for a group of school kids. "You don't need to say any more."

Lisa paused momentarily, reflecting on the priest's humility. "Father Byron, I'm not much good at casual conversation. May I speak frankly?"

The priest nodded with a look in his eyes that said there is really no time to do anything else. "Let's go inside. It's a bit damp out here."

Lisa followed the priest into a small, dimly lit foyer. A disturbing, life-size statue of St. Francis stared knowingly at her from the left, while an ancient Eastern Orthodox icon made its presence felt from a wall on the right. The priest led her through an open, sparsely furnished living area, down a darkened corridor, and into his faintly brighter study. The priest hung his parka on a coat tree behind a large antique desk at the far end of the room. Floor-to-ceiling bookcases lined the walls, interrupted only by a small fireplace, the mantel of which displayed two weathered photographs. On the left was Bede Griffiths, a Benedictine monk who lived the last years of his life as a Hindu renunciate in India; on the right was Sri Ramana Maharshi, the Hindu guru of Arunachala.

Father Byron stared at Lisa from behind the desk for what seemed to be too long. The light from the reading lamp before him blurred her vision of the contour of his face and upper torso. When he finally moved toward her, she saw a form that was tall and wiry. A gently weathered, bearded face housed deep-set, dark eyes that spoke simultaneously of suffering and some final resolution.

The priest caught Lisa's eyes with his own, giving her silent acknowledgment. "You said you wanted to speak frankly?"

Lisa took a deep breath. "Father Byron, my time in this world has run out. I feel like I'm being held here by the barest of threads. I'm at a point where I no longer have any interest in living." Lisa could tell the priest was taking her seriously. "I see a way out, though, and that's why I've come to you."

"I see." The heaviness of the moment hung in the air. The priest motioned for Lisa to sit down.

Having made his guest comfortable in one of two worn Queen Anne chairs, arranged to face one another across a handcrafted brass coffee table, the priest stood over her. "Would you care for a beer?"

Lisa smiled. With that simple question, the tension lifted. "Sure.

Thanks."

Some say that in the hours when eerie darkness is such that no thing dares to move, the ghosts of priests past from the Monkton parish of St James haunt the neighboring hillsides. Perhaps a trifling story, but Lisa could have sworn she saw the shadow of a face staring coldly through the windowpane of the study. It was there and then gone.

The priest returned with two pint glasses brimming with beer. He seemed to be in some silent prayer, holding the tray before her. "In England, they call this half-and-half. Half Guinness Stout and half Harp's Lager. The lager is poured in first, and then the Guinness is carefully layered on top. The difference in the specific gravities of the two allows the Guinness to float on the lager."

Lisa laughed. "Wow, you sure know your beer."

The priest smiled sheepishly. "Well, let's just say that beer like this is considered to be food itself. It's not just some liquid one consumes with food."

The priest stared meaningfully at his guest. They both knew that shortly they would be speaking of serious things that may very well take them to the loneliest place there is.

5

Father Byron rhythmically swirled the half-and-half in his official British government-certified pub glass. He seemed infinitely satisfied with his lot in life. "You say your time in this world has run out. Is there some *other* world where you see yourself being more comfortable?"

Lisa Browning smirked. "None that I know of." She felt a heaviness in her fifty-one-year-old body: a five-foot-five-inch frame attractively carrying 140 pounds. Her big, lazy, blue eyes were housed comfortably in a wide, pretty, peaches-and-cream-complected face.

"Is there nothing in this world that stimulates your will to live? Can you deny that love and beauty and creativity coexist with tragedy and suffering?"

"I don't deny it. I'm not even suffering. It's just that I have nothing left to give. I'm an empty shell."

The priest stroked his short-cropped beard. "Have you given yourself in the past?"

Lisa looked away from the priest's eyes. Eyes that had given up long ago. Eyes that saw more of her than she could see herself. "Giving myself to one cause or another is what my life has always been about. As a teenager, I did volunteer work in a hospital. In high school and through my college years, I worked as a 'Big Sister.' Then, after college, I did a three-year stint in the Peace Corps. Then it was the Freeze movement. Then Amnesty International. Now I'm working four nights a week in a women's crisis center."

The priest's eyes were like polished mirrors. "Have you received no meaning or joy from this work?"

"Certainly. There have been times when I felt very good about my efforts. But I see now that the work is never finished. We can never do enough. Whatever work I've done has just evaporated into the prospective needs of the future."

The priest reflectively sipped his beer. "What you say is true, Lisa. You never can give enough. But this is the nature of life. It's always calling us to do more."

"And I have answered that call." Lisa caught the eyes of the priest with her own, and both could feel the pull of truth. "Father Byron, I'm not some silly adolescent. I'm fifty-one years old. I've given myself to serious causes and have exhausted myself in the process. I *know* who I am, and I know it's time to stop."

The priest cocked his head as if to summon forth some idea hitherto unconceived. "Lisa, I'm not unfamiliar with what you're going through. As a priest, I've come to understand what it means to lead a life of service. And for sure, there are moments when one has great doubts about whether it's all worth it. But I must tell you: you are not alone. There are people like you, people who have had enough, who nevertheless choose to continue on. They literally *outlive* themselves. They do what they do without any expectations, and somehow their capacity to give becomes boundless."

Lisa's smile and sharp, clear eyes told the priest that this description did not fit her. "Father Byron, I understand about giving. But I've seen something in myself that I cannot deny. I've seen that my life is over."

The priest tilted his half-and-half to the side, watching the frothy beer coat the pint glass. "What are you afraid of, Lisa?"

Lisa shrugged her shoulders. "I'm not afraid of anything. That's what I'm trying to tell you. I simply have no interest in living. The lack of interest is not even my choice."

The priest slugged down the last of his beer. "What exactly do you mean?"

Lisa took a deep breath and leaned forward. "As a child I had a recurring dream. Not a nightmare, just a very peculiar dream. I would be climbing a steep mountain slope. It was early morning, and a thick mist made it difficult to see. Suddenly I would reach the mountaintop, and there was a clearing. What I saw took my breath away! Walking in line, very slowly, was a group of old men. Their heads were shaved, and they wore dark maroon robes. They each carried a small lantern. As a child, of course, I didn't know what I was seeing. It wasn't until later that I realized these were Buddhist monks."

The priest sat very still. His nod told her to continue.

"At any rate, these monks would pass by me and with a simple glance, acknowledge my presence. The last monk, however, would stop before me. Holding his lantern in one hand, he would take my hand with the other. He had the gentlest touch imaginable. Then he looked into my eyes and spoke: *If you want to be free, you must give completely. That is all.* The monk began to walk away but then stopped. Then he said, *When all fear goes, you'll know it's time.*

Lisa's eyes filled with tears. The priest's eyes never left hers. "Please go on," he said.

"It probably sounds strange, but even as a little girl I knew what the monk meant. I *knew* what he meant. And I've lived that way. I really have given myself completely. What I didn't understand was the finality of it all. But that changed three months ago."

"What happened three months ago?"

23

"First, let me say that the dream stopped when I was twelve. As mysteriously as it came, it stopped. But three months ago, something happened, and now things are different."

Lisa paused as an uncanny awareness rushed through her consciousness: *How odd it is that my life had brought me to this precipice. It's as if some unseen hand has pushed me along to this point of no return.* She looked at Father Byron. He sat so very still. Anchored in some deep space.

"Three months ago, I took a trip to Sri Lanka. I have an interest in Buddhism, so I wanted to experience South Asia. I stayed a few days at a Buddhist monastery in the mountains of Nuwara Eliya, just outside the city of Kandy. One morning I got up very early, meditated with the monks, and then hiked up a steep hill in the morning mist. I'd never seen such a morning. The sun barely showing itself in the east, the moon hanging high in the dark blue sky in the west, the mist swirling in the soft breeze. I was overcome by the simple grandeur of it all. And then it happened: I reached the tree line, and a clearing opened up before me. The swirling mist was heavy, and the reflected light from the emerging sun gave off a mysterious, orange glow. Something pulled my gaze to the left—and out of the orange-glowing mist appeared a group of old monks walking in line with their lanterns. My brain completely froze. I couldn't process anything that was happening. I was just part of the happening.

"As the monks passed by, each turned his head to me in acknowledgment. And then the last monk stopped before me. He held his lantern in one hand and took my hand with the other. His touch was gentle but firm. He looked straight into my eyes. Then he spoke: *You have given yourself well, played your part well. Believe me when I tell you that all of this is nothing but a dream. You are a character in this dream. You have fulfilled your duty as this character. There is nothing more for you to do. It's time for you to go. It's not only okay, it's necessary. You will soon know what I mean.* The monk let go of

24

my hand, placed his lantern on the ground, and bowed deeply before me. At that point, my mind exploded. I began to weep uncontrollably, and by the time I regained my composure, he was gone. There was nothing but the mist and the cool morning air."

Father Byron stared at Lisa from somewhere beyond space and time. "Okay, I understand."

"You do? You *really* do?"

"Yes, I understand."

"Ever since that monk bowed to me, I've had no personal desire to live. I feel that it's time to die, that it's the right thing to do. He said I would soon know what he meant. Now I do."

Father Byron stood up, walked to the study window, and stared out into the evening darkness. "For some of us, dreams can be the gateway to self-understanding. Dreams that carry self-revelatory messages are personalized myths. They really do touch a sacred, unconscious part of us."

The priest looked at Lisa with a still, empty gaze. "I can't tell you what to do. It doesn't work that way. Life pulls and pushes us. It's folly to think you can resist the pulling and pushing. The foolish imagine the movements of life to be a consequence of free will. The wise know it is destiny. That's what the monk was telling you."

Lisa thoughtfully sipped her beer. "It's destiny. There's no other way to understand it."

The priest stood still as a statue. "Do you know what Camus said about suicide? He said it was cowardly. That it was unacceptable."

"Do you believe that?" Lisa asked with a sting in her voice.

"It doesn't matter what I believe."

"It does to me!"

"I do not *believe* in anything," the priest said softly. "Life is not something that can be captured in the straightjacket of belief systems. Life has its own mysterious momentum—it doesn't cater to any of our beliefs. If you think you know which way it's going, you've lost touch with it altogether." The priest paused momentarily. "Even your belief that suicide is an answer puts you off course."

"I don't see suicide as an answer. This isn't about suicide. It's about destiny. You even said so yourself."

The priest was silent. *You're right*, he thought. *You've passed the test.*

Lisa wiped her lips with the back of her hand. "Something else happened yesterday afternoon. I was hiking in Robert E. Lee Park. After about an hour, I lay down to rest under some trees. I fell asleep. The next thing I know, I'm awake and surrounded by a pack of dogs. There must have been a dozen of them. They were moving all over me. I cautiously got up and started walking to my car. One by one, the dogs lost interest—except for one. This one dog was different. There was something meanspirited about it. It stalked me for twenty or thirty yards, growling and baring its teeth. It was as if this dog and I were meant to confront one another. Like something necessary was being played out."

The priest returned to his chair and sat down. He stared at her, unsurprised.

"What happened next makes me wonder about my sanity. The dog, or whatever it was, *spoke* to me. Or, more correctly, something spoke *through* it. The voice coming through that animal was otherworldly. It said it wanted to kill me."

The priest stroked his beard. He was taking her seriously.

"What I did in response astounded me: I stared the creature down. I showed it I would not be intimidated. I showed it I was not afraid. And then I heard a voice coming through my body. It was as if I were witnessing a staged scene. The voice channeling through me told the creature that I didn't care what it did to me! That I was dead already."

The priest concentrated on what she said with intensity. He nodded silently.

"What's interesting about this is that I've always been *terrified* of dogs. I mean totally freaked-out *terrified*. I don't know why. It's as if the fear were wired into my personality at birth. But yesterday, I wasn't afraid. I wasn't afraid at all. I was cautious but completely calm."

The priest looked at her intently, eyes squinting. "And what do you attribute this calmness to?"

"From my reading of Buddhism, I've learned that fear is the last attachment to go. When you no longer fear anything, the personal self is dissolved. That's what the monk was telling me in my dream." Lisa drained the last of her beer. "I knew yesterday afternoon my life had come to an end. The monk on the mountain top forecast it."

The priest stared at her silently.

"Father Byron, I didn't come here hoping you would change my mind."

The priest sat straight up, as if suddenly awakened from a deep sleep. "I wouldn't think of changing your mind. You know that already. Otherwise, you would have had this discussion with Father Welch."

Lisa smiled. "I suppose you're right."

The priest winked at her. "I suppose I am."

Silence permeated the room. The priest leaned forward in his chair. He spoke with a softness that was certitude itself: "I hope you know how blessed you are. Life has revealed to you some of its greatest mysteries. This does not happen often. And when it does, it is usually misunderstood. The messages are wasted. The opportunity is missed. We'll see what you do with it."

With this pronouncement anything that could be interpreted as perfunctory came to an end. Lisa understood, perhaps for the first time, that she was on her own. The priest was a clean mirror in which she could see herself projected toward the unknown.

The priest rubbed his tired eyes. "It's late. What I'd like you to do is digest what we've said here tonight. If you wish to continue, come and see me again tomorrow evening. Let's say around seven."

Looking into her eyes, he knew her return was imminent. Two souls would walk an existential tightrope over what some might call a moral abyss.

6

The grandfather clock in the hallway outside the study struck midnight. By this time the priest had switched to scotch. Sitting behind his desk, sipping systematically on the Glenfiddich, he *witnessed* his mind ponder the evening's strange conversation. Ever since his experiences in Bali, his mind functioned as if driven by an unseen hand. He no longer saw his thoughts as his own. They appeared and disappeared in his mind like clouds coming and going in the empty sky. Something within him *witnessed* the thoughts. He was often entertained and sometimes surprised by what was written across the open sky of his consciousness.

The problem of human meaning and redemption is a common specter haunting anyone who reflects on the significance of his or her life. But Lisa Browning is blessed. Very few would see and understand this. The common man would say that so much life lies ahead. The truth is that this soul has tasted a drop of nectar from destiny's fruit. Riddles of long-ago dreams are illuminated in the waking state. Pure grace is moving her to the end of her journey.

I cannot tell her, in good conscience, that what she proposes to do is in some way wrong or evil. Those categories of understanding and explanation have been left behind long ago. Life has somehow brought her to this point, and she is facing a decision that everyone faces, if only unconsciously: **do I live life through, or do I abort it?** *Only here, the abortion is the living through. In Lisa, there is no pathology that, given the chance to heal, would later turn to thanksgiving. Her soul has simply sailed into port.*

Moving across the room to warm himself by the fireplace, the priest looked into the eyes of his mentors on the mantelpiece and recognized again, as he had so many times before, that the light coming from the windows of their souls would serve to illuminate but not dictate.

These were teachers who pulled away the props from beneath one's superstructure of convention and conditioning. Their message was one of self-abandonment: *give yourself to the mystery of life, and allow life's native intelligence, its native energy, to function through you!*

This is what these visionaries had taught him: his own possessive intelligence was too small, too petty, too conditioned by the inherited prejudices of the ages to see into, much less understand, the mysteries of life and love and, yes, evil and horror as well. Only by casting off the limited, egocentric intelligence and the insidious conceit of knowledge that it engenders could one open oneself to life (some would say God) and its vast ambiguities and paradoxes and indecipherable displays of grace. Only by offering oneself to life and *trusting* life, can one be picked up and used as an instrument of that unfathomable intelligence.

I am just here. Innocence in the midst of the great becoming that is life. I am moved about and play my part in the natural course and flow of this majestic drama. With an enduring trust in life, a trust that goes beyond any rational explanation, I no longer interfere with the happening.

Lisa Browning has come to me. I offered no invitation. She has come to me as she moves along some dark corridor leading to the end of life as she knows it. Who knows why or how it happens this way?

The priest stared into his glass of scotch. The libation displayed caramel swirls of softness in the hard crystal glass. The swirls reminded him of Lisa's movement of fate. The priest closed his eyes in a calm perspicacity that would send lesser minds into guilt's sustained oblivion.

7

Hillary Miles was not imagining things. There *was* someone knocking softly at her apartment door. She squinted at the alarm clock. "Jesus, it's two a.m.," she mumbled. She got up, found her glasses, put on her robe, and made her way to the front door. After seeing who it was through the peephole, she turned the lock and let him in.

"My God, what are you doing here? It's two in the morning."

"I had to see you," he said softly.

Clad in fashionable trench coat and hat, he put his arm around her and led her toward the bedroom.

8

Lisa Browning walked across the Johns Hopkins Homewood campus. She enjoyed the silence of the early morning hours, especially after the long rain the evening before. The leaves were wet and soft beneath her boots, and the dawn's pink light welcomed the delicate voices of birds creating nature's symphony.

Lisa Browning was in love with the *present moment*. She knew this beyond all doubt. And she knew why. It was because her life was over. There were no more fanciful dreams, no more expectations, no more fears, no more failures. Nothing of the pain of impermanence could touch her. She stopped walking, stood very still, took a deep breath, closed her eyes, and turned within: *There is joy in the glistening colors of the wet leaves. There is joy in the evening that beckons. There is joy in the anticipation of what lies beyond.*

Lisa pulled open the heavy door at the entrance to Levering Hall, breezed across the expansive, dimly lit foyer, and climbed the stairs with an uncanny faith that defied the darkness. She entered the second floor corridor, made a right, then a left, and arrived at the familiar door embossed with the title **OFFICE OF THE CHAPLAIN**. She took her key from her blazer pocket. As she inserted it in the lock, the door fell open.

Lisa growled, "What the hell?"

Hunched over in the dark hallway, she could see the lock had been broken and the door jimmied open. Entering the office with circumspection, she flipped the light switch on the wall adjacent to the door. The overhead fluorescent lights came on slowly, one at a time, and illuminated bits and pieces of the large outer office much as binoculars bring a fuzzy landscape into focus.

Things appeared to be in order. The outer office was as she had left it Friday evening. Lisa calmly approached the door leading to the chaplain's private office. She turned the handle. It didn't budge. *Good.* Then she walked across the room toward her own office. She knew what she would find before she got there. Her door had been jimmied. She cautiously pushed it open and flicked on the lights.

The office was not ransacked. In fact, her first glance told her nothing was out of order. The only items of value in the office were the Staffordshire dogs crowning the mantelpiece over the old, defunct fireplace and the gold, antique pocket watch perched in its glass case on her desk. These treasures had not been touched.

It struck her as odd that *her* office had been targeted. *What could anyone want from her office?*

The drawers of her desk had been broken into, but none of her personal belongings had been taken. Making her way to the file cabinet in the back corner of the office, she was surprised to see what the intruder had been after. Files had been removed from the cabinet and were lying open on the floor in the corner.

Lisa's mind was humming. She was having trouble understanding what those files could possibly contain that would be of interest to anyone. All that was there were project statements for various social service jobs and some recently completed reports on volunteer workshops dealing with inner city illiteracy and prisoner education.

As she rummaged through the papers and files scattered on the floor, it dawned on her, with uncanny certainty, that what the intruder was looking for were the personal files of students she was counseling. Part of Lisa's job as assistant to the chaplain was serving as the director of Student Life, which sometimes involved amateur psychological sleuthing into the dark corridors of the student psyche. Lisa was like a great listening sponge. She didn't solve dilemmas—

she lessened their intensity. The personal counseling files, however, were not kept in the file cabinet. They were kept under lock and key in the bottom left drawer of Lisa's desk. Lisa could see from where she was standing that the drawer was open, but she could not remember what she had seen in that drawer when she hastily checked the desk a few minutes earlier.

9

By the time her secretary arrived, Lisa was talking to Captain Gregory Swenson of the Hopkins Campus Police. Swenson was a short, squat, black man with a gut that spoke of too many beers and egg rolls. His gun belt sagged low on his hips, and his eyeglasses were perched on top of his bald head. With a tired-out Southern drawl, he said, "I'll need the names of the students."

Lisa shook her head. "I don't know if I should give them to you. I've promised the students confidentiality."

"I can't investigate the break-in if I don't have the names."

Lisa smirked. "Well, I'll think about it. Can't you dust for fingerprints or something?"

Captain Swenson rolled his eyes. "Lady, that only happens in the movies."

10

"Detective Linda Barnes," she said as she waved her shield at the apartment superintendent and entered the crime scene. Three uniformed Baltimore City police officers were standing in the middle of the living room, talking. "What gives?" Barnes said to none of them in particular.

One of the officers approached her. "Hey, Detective. Looks like we've got a homicide here. The body's in the bedroom." The officer pulled a notepad from his breast pocket and referred to what he had written. "The victim's name is Hillary Miles. She was a nineteen-year-old Hopkins student. It looks like she lived here alone, and whoever did her didn't have to break the door down. No signs of forced entry. When she missed an exam this morning, a friend of hers got worried and had the super open the place up."

Detective Barnes took the officer's version of the story in stride. Just another day's work. Just another mess to clean up after. Cleaning-up-after was different from cleaning up. Cleaning up a case ended with some kind of closure; cleaning-up-after left a sour taste in one's mouth that didn't go away. Detective Barnes knew that the latter was more prevalent than the former.

The officer glanced up from his notepad. "One other thing. Whoever did it locked the door behind him when he left."

"Him?" Barnes asked sarcastically.

"You know what I mean."

"Have you called the lab techs?"

"Yeah. They're on their way."

"Okay. Tell the super to hang around. I'll want to talk to him."

Barnes entered the bedroom. The window shades of the eighth-story apartment were raised, and the midafternoon sun flooded the room. It was obvious that there had been no struggle. The room was obsessively tidy.

"What's happened here?" Barnes asked the police pathologist who was examining the body on the bed.

The pathologist, Dr. Vernon Plitt, grunted with back pain as he pulled his knee off the bed. "Looks to me like she was suffocated with one of these pillows. The bruises on her face are consistent with something like that. Won't know for sure, though, until we examine her back at the lab."

Barnes stared at the body splayed across the bed. "Turn the data around fast, Plitt. Give me half a chance at solving this one."

Plitt scratched his bare, bloated belly protruding between two lower buttons of his stained white shirt. "You know what they say, Barnes. Quid pro quo. Quid pro quo."

11

Lisa Browning dialed the extension and punched on the speakerphone. "Captain Swenson? Hi, this is Lisa Browning. I've decided to release those names to you."

"It must be my lucky day," Swenson answered.

"You got paper and pen there? Okay, here goes: Robert McCann...Bill Berg...Ray Walsh...and Hillary Miles."

"Okay, Lisa. I'll get working on it." There was a long silence. "Hey, Lisa, aren't you going to wish me luck?"

"Good luck, Swenson. For some reason I think you're going to need it."

12

As she drove to Father Byron's, Lisa Browning was engulfed in a palpable silence—the kind of silence signifying great resolve. It was as if all had been decided long before. The thread of time and space holding her to this life was fraying, and she was letting go without resistance or regret.

Navigating the final serpentine leg of the lengthy driveway, Lisa reflexively applied the brake to avoid striking the priest who seemed to materialize out of thin air.

Father Byron, wearing a handsome tweed jacket, was returning from an early evening walk. A long, colorful, Burberry scarf flowed about his neck and shoulders. Greeting Lisa with a wave of his hand, he seemed unruffled at the near miss of the Volvo.

Lisa Browning rolled down the driver's side window. "Father Byron, please forgive me. You seemed to pop up out of nowhere. I hope I didn't frighten you."

Father Byron smiled sheepishly. "Oh, I'm fine. I do tend to appear and disappear without warning...at least, that's what people tell me." The priest pointed toward the house. "Park up around the bend by the front door."

Father Byron led his wayfaring friend into the house, and together they headed directly to the liquor cabinet in his study. The priest pulled out a bottle of Duff-Gordon No. 28. "I always find a glass of sherry to be especially delightful after a brisk walk in the countryside. Will you join me?"

"Sure. Thank you," Lisa answered. She wondered if the priest were an alcoholic.

After the sherry was poured and both were settled in the Queen Anne chairs situated around the brass coffee table, the priest looked at Lisa with a penetrating stare which she returned in kind. The soul communicates through the eyes, and there was no doubt that an understanding beyond words was presently shared. This was a woman who, in her fifty-one years, had seen her life reflected in the pure mirror of her soul. She had chosen to die unto this life, to no longer be of it or in it. The priest had made a similar choice many years ago, with the distinction that he had chosen to remain in it. They, in their respective ways, had both let go and were at peace.

The priest finally spoke. "When you really let go of life and simply allow it to happen, you learn to befriend silence and stillness."

Lisa smiled. "I know."

The priest sipped his sherry. "What exactly do you want from me?"

Lisa leaned forward, closed her eyes, and took a deep breath. When she returned her glance to the priest, he saw deep resolve in her eyes. "Father Byron, tomorrow morning I'm going to commit suicide. I'm not doing it because I'm angry or hurt, and not because I'm tortured by the prospect of continuing with my life. It isn't even a choice that I'm making—it feels more like the choice is being made for me. I'm just carrying out the order."

The priest smiled knowingly. "It's your destiny to do so."

"Yes. It's my destiny to do so."

Lisa rose from her chair and walked to the study window. *Had she seen that ghost once again, eyeing the proceedings from beyond the other shore?* She looked out the window into the evening blackness. "What I'm asking you to do is find my body, report my death to the police, and give my relatives and friends a simple, thoughtful farewell on my behalf." She turned and looked at the priest. "You can just say that the two of us were friends, that we had planned to have breakfast together at my apartment, and that you found me."

The priest shook his head. "You want me to act as if I knew nothing of your plans for suicide? What about your family? Do they have any suspicion of what you're going to do? I know I don't want to deceive them."

"You won't have to. I've composed letters to all my significant others. Just see that they get them, if you would. I'll leave them out where you can find them. I'll also leave money for the cremation and some instructions on how I would like the funeral service conducted. All you have to do is find me and do what comes naturally."

The priest absorbed all that was said—and yet seemed to float above it. He cocked his head in response to the sound of a phone ringing in a distant room. "Excuse me, I'll be right back."

Lisa turned to the window and gazed out into the darkness. *There certainly were ghosts out there. She could feel them. Just a lingering presence, a residue of psychic energy. Her reflection in the pane of glass was ghost-like, too. A premonition of the other side?*

The priest ducked his head into the study. "Duty calls. Hospice work. I have to go."

Lisa felt the presence of deep compassion. "May I walk you to your car? I have one other thing to ask you."

13

Lisa Browning and Father Byron huddled next to Father Byron's Mercedes. A stiff wind carried a chill from the evening dampness.

"Father Byron, do you believe in ghosts?"

The priest looked at her quizzically. "Why in the world do you ask?"

"Because I think your hillside is haunted. I think you have ghosts all around here."

Father Byron sighed. "You *are* a prescient one! Yes, ghosts *do* haunt this hillside." Father Byron chuckled as he searched his coat pocket for his car key. "The ghosts are what's left of the priests of St. James Parish. But that's another story altogether." Byron unlocked his car door. "Not to worry. I won't be joining them. When I die, I'll have other fish to fry."

Lisa hugged herself against the frigid elements. "Well, I just wanted you to know that I *felt* them. The ghosts. They peer through your study window."

Father Byron opened the car door. "Yes, I know they're there. You are one of only two people who have ever felt their presence, other than me." The priest stood motionless, lost in a mood of contemplation. "Lisa, how are you going to do it?"

Lisa smiled with resolve as she handed him the key to her apartment. "Not to worry. It won't be gory."

14

Frank Justin held the priest's hand for what would be the last time. "Well, Father, I'm afraid you can't do much this time. I'm on my way out."

The priest smiled. "I think you're right, Frank. The flaps are down, and you're coming in for a landing."

Frank laughed gently to prevent another coughing spasm. "God, I used to love flying those planes." He closed his eyes and swallowed. *It hurt to swallow.* "You know, my mind has remained clear through all of it. It's just the damn body. It quit on me."

"When it wants to quit, it quits."

The eyes looking out through that sallow, drawn face had so many questions. "You know, the last time I thought I was dying, you did something to me. We never really talked about it. I guess I really didn't want to."

"You did it, Frank. Not me."

Frank's grip tightened, then relaxed. The unshaven face took the shape of a smile. "Don't give me that. You think I don't know? I was lying here, dying—what was it? Three years ago? And you came in here and sat with me and talked to me, but the whole time you were looking at me in a funny kind of way. I saw the look—like you were seeing straight inside my bones, like you were sizing up the cancer there. Then you placed your hand on my forehead. After that I don't know what happened. When I woke up, you were gone, and I was feeling better. And hell, I went home three days later. You know what the hospice workers say about you? They say you're some kind of shaman or mystic."

"Frank, I'm just pleased you lived another three years."

"Me too, Father."

The priest used a tissue to wipe some spittle from Frank's lips. "It's going to be all right, Frank. You're right on schedule."

"Thanks for being here. It helps. Could you stay a while longer?

"Absolutely. I'm here."

Two minutes later, a bright white light emanated from Frank's body and filled the room with the wonder of the infinite. Father Byron felt the light surge through his own body like a pulse of electricity.

15

He stood alone in his handsome Brooks Brothers trench coat and Stetson Winston hat at the entrance of the Hopkins House apartment building in Guilford. The night's dark shadows mixed with the silvery glow from the streetlamps to wash the building's light gray bricks with an airy watercolor motif. The neighborhood was extraordinarily quiet and still.

He carefully checked the bordering streets for the Volvo. It wasn't there. He took the stairs, rather than the elevator, to the sixth floor. Lisa Browning. Number 618. He listened attentively at the door. When he heard no sounds coming from inside, he easily defeated the lock with an expired credit card, entered the foyer, and quickly closed the door behind him.

A single table lamp burned dimly in the living room. Carefully securing the revolver in his gloved hand, he quietly made his way through the apartment. No one was there. His heart beat like a jackhammer, and for the briefest of moments, he considered abandoning his mission. All that went by the wayside, however, when his eye caught something peculiar on the glass coffee table.

There was a systematic arrangement of envelopes and letters neatly placed in vertical rows on the table. Names and addresses were on the envelopes, and beneath the flaps were the letters to be placed within them. At the edge of the table sat a green plastic prescription bottle. He carefully placed the handgun on the black leather couch, twisted the cap off the bottle, and counted six tiny pink pills along the curve of its base. *No label on the bottle.* He replaced the top and returned the bottle to its original position. *What about the letters?* When he saw what they contained, a wide smile spread across his face. It was as if some inexplicable good fortune had fallen from the heavens. With his heart lightened, he grabbed the gun and began to make his way to the door. But something stopped him cold. The sound of the turning doorknob was like an unexpected explosion. He slid up close to the wall meeting the key-shaped foyer entrance. A howling scream from his heart signaled the unthinkable.

16

The priest sat in his study, witnessing the reverie of contemplation that sometimes overtook him.

Destiny—what an odd trick for God to play on us. It seems so clear that we are individuals with free will. We feel responsible for what we do or fail to do. We take everything so personally—desire, anger, fear, and guilt are testimony to that. But if the truth be known, free will is the grand illusion. The divine hypnosis. The truth of this life is that there is no free will. Our feelings of responsibility, desire, anger, fear, and guilt are illusory passions.

The mind/body complex with which we identify comes into this world predetermined. We have a specific genetic coding; we are born into a specific family and social context; we undergo specific patterns of conditioning. None of it is our choice. None of it is our responsibility. Our modern science of brain functioning has revealed that our responses to stimuli from the outside world, as well as to stimuli from our own inner world of thoughts and emotions, are automatic— they're reflexive. Our actions simply happen! And then a fraction of a second later, we claim them as our own. That's the illusion! That's the divine hypnosis!

*As individuals, we think this life is about **each one of us**. But it is not. This life is about the **functioning of the totality**. We all are playing a part in the functioning, but the sense of it all lies in the totality. We think we are doing all of this, but in fact **we are made to do all of this.***

*The totality of the life force is moving its way to completion (whatever that means!), and our finite, concept-ridden minds simply cannot grasp the meaning of it. That realization is the uncanny wisdom that brings peace to the heart. Things are happening, but **no one** is* *responsible. It's all a dream in the mind of God. When one really understands this, desire, fear, anger, and guilt just drop away. There is action and acceptance, action and acceptance. Peace in action. Action in peace.*

17

Linda Barnes woke with a hangover. She had been up late the night before, drinking Glenlivet and reading Edith Wharton's *The Age of Innocence*. Linda liked reading the book on which a film is based before she saw the movie. She also liked single malt scotch.

After showering and dressing, she enjoyed a cup of coffee while listening to Mahler's First Symphony on her tape deck. Linda had lived in this apartment for six years, and it fit her like a glove. The rooms were small and scantly furnished, with an emphasis on open space rather than possessions. She loved the generous picture windows that opened every room of the apartment to the outside world. During the morning hours, when sunlight poured through these windows, billions of dust particles danced and shimmered in the air. And because she lived on the eighth floor, with no other high-rises within blocks, she needed no blinds or curtains on the windows. Looking out her windows, over the vast expanse of the Mount Washington community below, she was reminded of what freedom must be like for a soaring bird, light and high in the open sky.

On this particular morning, Barnes went straight to the Hopkins registrar's office to get any information she could on the Miles girl before going to see the medical examiner at precinct headquarters.

18

Father Byron. Sipping coffee in his study. Gazing out the window. The leaves had fallen from most of the trees, and grayness enveloped everything. The pregnant stillness, the barren landscape, the haunting specter of the ticking grandfather clock reminded him of where he had to go and what he had to do and what he would find. The books surrounding him purported to contain so much wisdom but in the end probably amounted, as Aquinas said of his own work, to not much more than straw.

Byron walked to the bookcase and pulled out T.S. Eliot's *Little Gidding*. He turned to the familiar passage as he had done so many times before:

> *We shall not cease from exploration*
> *And the end of all our exploring*
> *Will be to arrive where we started*
> *And know the place for the first time.*

He wondered if Lisa were conscious of where she was.

19

The priest pulled into a parking space on Cloverhill Road and walked across 39th Street. He stood for a moment, looking up at the twelve-story apartment building. He thought of his time in Bali. *The mystery of the sights, sounds, colors, fragrances. He remembered surrendering to God. The surrender was done in good conscience, although then, he never could have imagined what it truly meant. Now he knew it meant being in the world but not of it—moving about on a stage in a world-drama that was not of his making. He was a puppet in the hands of God. Compassionate action and acceptance were his only strings.* He took the elevator to the sixth floor and went straight to apartment 618. He searched his coat pocket for the key Lisa had given him, slipped the key into the lock, and opened the door.

The apartment was dark and silent and completely still. He turned on the light in the foyer. In the dim disbursal of illumination, he saw, ever so slightly, the silhouette of a body on the black leather couch in the room before him. His legs felt heavy, and he had to command them to move. There was an odd smell, which he recognized as death. Moving forward, he cautiously switched on the table lamp next to the couch.

Lying before him was the body. But it was all wrong. He *knew* it was all wrong.

Lisa Browning lay twisted on one end of the couch. A bullet hole gaped from the side of her forehead. Her eyelids were not entirely closed, and the eyes that floated there told a macabre story with their cold and lifeless stare. A revolver dangled from one of her hands.

The priest slowly backed away from the body and the flotsam of blood and brains that splattered the wall behind it. He sat down in a chair across the room. Breathing deeply, head in his hands, he tried to clear his mind. *Lisa had said, "Not to worry...it won't be gory." Something has gone wrong here. Something has gone very wrong.*

Father Byron raised himself from the chair and walked over to the coffee table. Envelopes and letters were organized in rows on the table. He glanced at a few of the letters and saw that they were the suicide notes to family members and friends. It was curious, though. Why were the letters not put into the envelopes and sealed? These were confidential and personal musings, Lisa's last and final communications to a few special people. She would not have left these letters and notes lying about indiscriminately.

Byron quickly surveyed the rest of the apartment. He found no instructions for him to carry out and no money for the funeral expenses. Looking at the body one more time, he was sure. This was no suicide. In a voice that was dry and far away, he heard himself say, *"God, Almighty, what has happened here?"*

20

A uniformed patrolman was the first to arrive. Byron had called the police just as Lisa had requested. After a cursory examination of the body, the patrolman told Byron to touch nothing. He then walked circumspectively throughout the entire apartment, looking for something or nothing in particular, and recorded a few details in a small notebook.

"I've got to ask you a few questions," the officer said to Byron, who was standing at the sixth-floor window silently watching the traffic weave up and down 39th Street.

"I understand," Byron said mechanically.

"What brought you here this morning?"

"Lisa and I had planned to have breakfast." Byron said this without thinking. It was as if he were standing outside his body, watching himself speak. All he knew was that, for the time being, he would just give the party line as he had been requested to do.

"Can you give me her full name?"

"Yes. Lisa Browning."

"How long have you known her?"

"Only a few days." Byron pointed toward the notes on the table. "Those letters are suicide notes."

The officer ambled to the table, took a cursory look, and returned to Byron's side. "Did she strike you as suicidal?"

"No." Byron's mind was beginning to clear, and he knew this charade was going to catch up with him sooner or later.

The officer looked at his notes. "What's the spelling of your last name?"

"My name is Byron. Father Byron. B-Y-R-O-N."

The officer raised his eyebrows and quickly surveyed Byron from head to toe. "Don't you guys wear collars anymore?"

Byron, who was again staring out the window, shook his head *no*.

The officer meandered to the front door. Not in any particular hurry. He eyeballed the inside doorknob. Then he opened the door, and like a skilled carpenter, ran his fingers down its side—paying particular attention to the retractable latch. "Father Byron, when you got here, was the door open?"

Byron shrugged his shoulders. "No. I had a key."

"She gave it to you?"

"She gave it to me last night. She said to use it if she was out buying pastries when I arrived." Byron startled himself by his talent for deception.

The officer pursed his lips and stared dubiously at Byron. "I'm calling in a homicide detective."

Byron turned away from the window and looked at the officer for what seemed to be too long. "I think that would be appropriate."

21

Captain Gregory Swenson waited patiently in the Hopkins registrar's office. Twenty-four hours ago, he had issued formal requests to obtain both personal and academic records on the four students identified by Lisa Browning. Now he was ready to see the goods.

An administrative assistant, with a stick-figure body and a startling shock of short, red hair, suddenly appeared with a stack of printouts. "I've got the records for McCann, Berg, and Walsh. Identifying information and stuff like that...and also some of the academic material...major, department chair, advisor, and stuff like that." The young woman talked very fast and appeared out of breath.

Swenson just wanted to grab the printouts from her and get out of there, but she was holding the documents close to her chest with a kind of possessiveness that was intimidating.

"Now we have a problem with Miles," said the administrative assistant. "It's a rather delicate situation."

"What's the problem?" Swenson asked halfheartedly.

"The problem is...well, the problem is she's dead."

Swenson turned his head sideways. A sarcastic smile spread across his wide, glistening face. "Dead? What do you mean...'dead'?"

The administrative assistant pursed her lips in an officious manner. "She was found dead in her apartment yesterday afternoon. A police detective was here early this morning asking for information on her."

Swenson winced and rubbed his eyes with the stubby thumb and index finger of his left hand. His right hand was perched on his right hip, adjacent to his prodigious beer belly. "How did she die?"

"I don't know. Nobody's saying anything right now."

"I think I better have a conversation with this detective. Do you remember his name?"

"The detective is a woman."

"A woman?"

"Yeah, a woman. Do you want her name or don't you?"

Swenson stared at his interlocutor. *Christ,* he thought, *does it have to be this difficult?* "Yeah, I want her name."

"Barnes, Detective Linda Barnes."

22

The Baltimore City Police medical examiner's office was small and dingy. Yellowed concrete walls surrounded a metal desk piled high with autopsy reports and old newspapers. Two straight-backed, wooden chairs sat in front of the desk. The air was palpably thick, permeated by too many years of smoke generated by the skunky Dunhill tobacco that Dr. Plitt burned obsessively in his broken-down corncob pipes. The stinky residue of the smoke merged disagreeably with the oppressive, lingering odor of formaldehyde.

When Detective Barnes entered the office, Dr. Plitt was sitting at his desk, studying *The Daily Racing Form.*

"That looks like interesting reading," Barnes said sarcastically.

Plitt looked up from the *Racing Form* and wrinkled his nose. He leaned back in his chair, hands behind his head, and smiled. "Well, Barnes, what can I do for you this fine morning?"

"I think you know, Plitt."

Plitt pursed his lips together and looked toward the ceiling. "Let me see. Could it have something to do with that little Hopkins coed we found the other day?"

"Come on, Plitt, I don't have all day. What did you find out?"

"What I found out, Barnes, is that the plot thickens." Plitt smiled sardonically as he paused in a suspenseful silence meant to irritate. Barnes just stared at him, nonplussed.

"Well, here we go," Plitt said mechanically. "Number one, the girl was suffocated with one of her own pillows. The saliva stains on the pillowcase tell the story. Number two, it took a pretty strong guy to take her out. She was struggling hard. We found a deep bruise on her chest, probably from the knee of her attacker. My guess is we're talking about a 185-to-200 pound man. Number three, the attacker didn't rape her. We found no semen, no vaginal or anal tearing. But what we did find was that this girl was pregnant. I'd say about five weeks."

Barnes shook her head and stared at the floor. "It's never clean, is it? Murder is bad enough. But murdering a pregnant woman...it's just too much."

An icy silence filled the room like that painfully still moment before an unavoidable, giant wall of water comes crashing down on an innocent and brittle figure playing in the surf.

"Anything else?" Barnes asked.

Plitt looked up from his desk. "Yeah. When you leave, close the door behind you."

23

The walk from Plitt's office to the detectives' squad room was one every homicide detective dreads when he or she knows they've been thrown a 'red ball'—a murder case with no witnesses, no evidence, no leads, and, ultimately, no luck. The lab techs would have a report on the fingerprint workup in a few days, but Barnes knew already that the well was dry. A veteran homicide detective has a sixth sense about a red ball. She knew this case was not going down.

When Barnes walked into the squad room, all the other detectives were out on the street. "Jesus, Louise," Barnes said to the lone secretary typing in a far corner of the office, "where the hell is everybody?"

The secretary looked up and shrugged her shoulders. She had a face that had grown hard after many years of working in this office of death. "There's a phone message on your desk."

Barnes picked up the scrap of paper. *Weds. 11 a.m. Call Captain Swenson of the Johns Hopkins Campus Police—555-2000.* She had no sooner finished reading the note, than the phone rang. "Homicide...Barnes," she barked into the receiver.

"Detective, this is Officer Cooley with the Sixth Precinct. I've got a body at the Hopkins House. Apartment 618. Possible suicide but homicide not ruled out."

"Okay, Cooley. I'm on my way." Barnes stuffed the phone message into the pocket of her jacket and moved swiftly out the door.

Driving north on Charles Street, Detective Linda Barnes decided she would finish *The Age of Innocence* in the next couple of nights and take in a matinee performance of the film at the Senator Theatre on

Sunday. A good book, a bottle of fine single malt scotch, a classic movie—these were the things that mattered to Linda Barnes. Being a cop pretty much washed out the rest of her life. She was an odd mixture of feminist intellectual, borderline alcoholic, sexual bon vivant, and contemplative recluse. She was smarter than any man she knew, could hold liquor better than any man she knew, and wanted sex with *no* man she knew. When it came to sex, she certainly had a healthy appetite, but wasn't going to waste it on boys who called themselves men. She hadn't met a man worthy of her in years.

Turning left on 39th Street, she began thinking about what she would find at the Hopkins House. *Another dead body. Death and more death. What kind of life had she carved out for herself?* She didn't want to think about it.

After parking her car on Cloverhill Road, she stared at herself in the rearview mirror. Her face was still attractive. But her eyes were tired and sad. She reached into her pocketbook, pulled out her brush, and ran it quickly through her short hair. She freshened her lipstick and got out of the car. Staring up at the twelve-story Hopkins House, she took a deep breath and started across the street.

Had she been more prescient, she might have seen the signs: the sun moving quickly from behind a cloud to the sky's open clearing, the sweep of a squadron of brightly colored finches diving in front of her and then away, the smell of early fall in the wind, the unexpected lightness in her step. All of these ciphers rushed her at once, but nothing in this world could have told her how the one she would encounter six stories up would change her life.

24

The name on the heavy, imposing oak door read:

Elliot Peachwater
Professor of Theology

Captain Swenson tried to compose himself before knocking. He felt intimidated by the highbrow professors at the University, and Peachwater was one whose reputation preceded him. After taking a deep breath, he nervously rapped on the door.

Instantly, from the depths of the room on the other side of the door, a loud, stylized voice bellowed, "Enter!"

Swenson slowly opened the heavy door into the large, ornate office of Professor Peachwater. Rich, colorful Persian rugs covered most of the parquet floor, and a dramatic Oriental tapestry woven of pure silk graced the wall that did not feature the professor's impressive library.

Peachwater was hovering over an unruly yucca plant next to his desk, copper watering can in one hand and textbook in the other. He was strikingly handsome: six feet tall, lean in body, clean shaven, silver haired, slightly tanned. He was dressed impeccably in a crisp, white, button-down shirt, dark burgundy tie, midnight blue cable waistcoat, pleated, dark brown tweed trousers, and wine-colored, tasseled loafers.

"You must be Captain Swenson," Peachwater said in his deep, melodious voice.

"Yes, sir. Thanks for seeing me."

"No problem. What can I do for you?"

"Did your secretary give you my message about Hillary Miles?"

"Just that you wanted to speak to me about her. What's happened? Is she in some kind of trouble?"

"Well, sir, I hate to be the one to tell you this, but she was found dead in her apartment Monday afternoon."

The pain in Peachwater's expression hung heavily around his mouth and eyes. "Oh, my God. I guess you know I was Hillary's advisor. I was very impressed with her. What in the world happened?"

"I don't know the details, sir. I've got a call in to the police detective working on the case. When she calls me back, I'll know more."

"Well, how can I help?"

"Well, I thought she might have talked to you about herself. You know, as her advisor, about any personal problems she might be having."

"What exactly do you mean by *personal* problems?" Peachwater asked with obvious interest.

"You know, if anybody was bothering her or harassing her." Both men stood silent. "You see, what bothers me is this—a few days before she died, a file on Hillary was stolen from the chaplain's office. She was undergoing some kind of counseling with Lisa Browning. She's the director of Student Life. Anyway, Browning wouldn't tell me what they talked about because she wanted to maintain confidentiality."

"I would think that a situation like this would require her to tell you about the counseling," Peachwater interrupted.

"Well, I plan to talk to her again. You can bet on that. Anyway, what can you tell me about Hillary? Did she ever confide in you?"

"No, I can't say that she did. Other than discussing academic matters, we mostly talked about philosophy and religion. She was very interested in thinking through traditional philosophical problems. So it was quite natural that we found each other's company enjoyable. But as far as her confiding in me, I'm afraid that never happened."

"I just can't help thinking that there must be some connection between the stolen file and her death," Swenson mused.

Peachwater nodded. "Maybe so. Well, if there's anything else I can help you with, don't hesitate to call." Peachwater had obviously had enough of Swenson and was already slipping into his stylish Brooks Brothers trench coat.

"Okay, Professor. Thanks for your help." Swenson moved toward the door, aware that he was no longer welcome.

Peachwater let some time pass between Swenson's departure and his own. Walking alone across the campus, anticipating his first martini of the afternoon at the Hopkins Club, he thought of Hillary Miles. By the time he reached the club, the tears in his eyes had cleared.

25

When Linda Barnes arrived at apartment 618, the uniformed officer was waiting at the door.

"Hey, Cooley."

"Hey, Detective. How's it going?"

"It's going. What do you have for me?"

Cooley shrugged his shoulders. "We've got a doozy in there. A middle-aged woman named Lisa Browning. Shot through the head. She left suicide notes, but it looks fishy to me." Cooley leaned into Barnes' personal space. Smirking. "And there's a priest inside who says he's her friend."

Barnes rolled her eyes. "Hold on a second. You say you think this is *not* a suicide?"

"I'm not sure, Detective. It looks suspicious to me."

"And what about the priest?"

"The priest is inside. He found her. He said he was supposed to have breakfast with her."

Barnes shook her head. Weary. "Fucking Catholics." Silence. "Okay. I'll take it from here."

Barnes walked into the apartment. The first thing she saw was the body. A lifeless, mutilated scarecrow at the end of the couch. She swallowed hard. Then, to her right, she saw a silhouette at the window, bathed in the bright morning sunlight. The man's back was to her. As she approached, he turned and their eyes met.

"Hi, I'm Detective Barnes." Looking into the eyes of the priest turned her inside out. She felt inexplicably weak and vulnerable.

"I'm Father Byron."

They stood still and silent, captured in some time warp where only the immediacy of the present survived. Both felt an uncomfortable and uncanny sense of destiny—as if two worlds, previously just missing each other, had finally come together.

"Tell me what happened," Barnes said.

The priest stroked his beard thoughtfully. "Lisa and I were to have breakfast together. When I arrived, this is what I found."

"Officer Cooley says this may have been a suicide."

Byron nodded. "There are suicide notes on the coffee table."

As Barnes turned and moved toward the coffee table, Byron was aching to tell her the truth. He knew he was moved by her. In fact, intensely attracted to her. But could he trust her? Was she interested in what really happened here—including his part in the plan gone awry—or was she the kind of cop who just sees what she wants to see and closes the case like a tidy box?

Barnes carefully surveyed the body and read bits and pieces of the suicide notes. She shook her head in puzzlement. "Father Byron, something bothers me about this. When I read these notes, I sense this woman was highly intelligent and very sensitive. Although, I must admit that committing suicide is a pretty insensitive thing to put your friends and family through. But when I look at the body and the gun, it just doesn't add up. I don't see her killing herself this way."

Byron. Silent. Too silent.

Barnes smiled coolly. "Father Byron, if you know more than you're telling me, you'd better fess up. I need to know everything I can about this case if I'm going to solve it." She paused and then said, "Look, maybe we should go down to headquarters, and have you give a formal statement."

Byron tried to size her up, but nothing came through. "All right. I'll talk to you. But I'd rather meet somewhere else."

Barnes shrugged her shoulders. "Where?"

"How about the Kent Lounge in Towson? Tonight. Around 8:30."

Barnes nodded involuntarily. "Okay. See you tonight." She looked at herself through her mind's eye. Why she was going along with this unconventional suggestion was beyond her comprehension. She felt as if she were being pushed by some unseen hand toward a place that may very well hold no safe harbor.

26

When Barnes got back to the squad room, she was tired and washed out. She hadn't eaten all day and knew it was not a good sign to crave scotch more than food. But that's the way it was.

After taking two Nuprin for her banging headache, she picked up the phone and called Captain Swenson.

"Captain Swenson? This is Detective Linda Barnes with the Baltimore City Police."

"Yeah. Detective Barnes, good to talk to you." Swenson was relieved that she had finally got back to him. "Look, I think we've got something fishy going on over here at the Hopkins campus. You know that Hillary Miles woman who was found dead in her apartment? Well, a couple of days before she died, a file on her was stolen from the chaplain's office. The director of Student Life, who works in that office, was counseling her on some personal problems."

"What kind of personal problems?" Barnes asked, suddenly interested.

"I don't know. The counselor wanted to maintain confidentiality. So she wouldn't tell me. But that was before Miles turned up dead."

"What's this counselor's name? I want to talk with her."

"Her name is Lisa Browning."

Barnes turned numb when she heard the name. "Hold it, hold it! What did you say her name is?"

"Lisa Browning." A heavy silence hung on the other end of the line.

"Hey, what do you know that you're not telling me?"

"Jesus, Swenson. This is too much. Look, I want you to do something for me. Get me the names and some identifying information on everyone on campus who was close to Miles. I've got to piece all this together somehow."

Swenson. Straightening his tie. Feeling tight in the chest. "I don't mind helping you, but you've got to let me in on what's going down. I'm working on this case too, you know."

"All right. Fair is fair. You have to understand that I can't share the details of the case with you. But I will tell you that Lisa Browning was found dead this morning."

"Oh, shit," Swenson crooned. "Man, oh, man, we got something going on down here."

"Yes, we do, Swenson. We surely do."

27

Linda Barnes parked her black Jeep in the vacant lot behind the Kent Lounge. A deep chill in the air harbored the scent of snow. When she opened the back door to the bar, the light, the music, the smoke, and all the scrambled voices of the patrons hit her at once. *She liked bars. Edgy.* She saw Byron sitting at a high-topped table in the corner. His tall, wiry body seemed to melt into the barstool. As she approached him, she could feel her large breasts being caressed by the fabric of her tight sweater.

"Hi, Father Byron."

The priest got up from the table and pulled out a barstool for her. "Please, call me Dick."

"Sure, Dick. You can call me Linda." *What is all this informality about?* she thought. *Strange.*

"Okay, Linda. What are you drinking?"

"I've been wanting scotch all day." She looked around, but no waiters or waitresses were in sight. "I think I'll go to the bar and order. Can I get you anything?"

Byron sipped his pint of Pete's Wicked Ale. "No, I'm fine."

Barnes waded through the crowd. When she got to the bar, she surveyed the collection of single malts. She hollered to the bartender, "I'll have a double Glenlivet on the rocks."

Glancing at Byron across the room, sitting quietly with his beer, she felt a girlish kind of exhilaration. *Jesus,* she thought, *I'm falling for a priest!* She shook her head quickly a few times, hoping she would snap out of it.

Making her way back to the table, maneuvering between bodies swaying in alcoholic daze, she kept her eye on him. There was no doubt that on some subliminal level, she felt connected to him. *But why?*

Sitting down at the table, she took a hit of scotch and leaned toward him. "Okay, Dick. What have you got for me?"

Byron stared at her for a moment, collecting his thoughts. "The first time I met Lisa Browning was this past Sunday evening. She came to my home, and together we embarked on a very odd conversation. She told me she was planning to commit suicide. She had her reasons. When I asked her what she wanted from me, she was very precise. She wanted me to discover her body, call the police, and make sure that her friends and relatives got the suicide notes that she had prepared. And finally, she asked me to conduct a simple memorial service. She said she would leave me money for the cremation and funeral expenses."

Silence. Barnes sensed that Byron wanted her to ask questions. "That's quite a story. Did you do or say anything to try to dissuade her?"

"From what? Suicide?"

Barnes nodded and took another hit of scotch.

"No. I interrogated her on why she had made this decision but didn't try to change her mind. I'm not into saving souls."

Barnes looked at him in disbelief. "I thought priests were supposed to save souls."

"Not this priest. If I had seen any immaturity or impulsiveness in her, not to mention some sign of insanity, I would not have agreed to take part in her plan. I certainly didn't do anything to encourage her. I just let her be."

"Oh, for God's sake!" Barnes barked with exasperation. "What the hell is going on here? A woman you have never met comes to you and tells you she is going to commit suicide. And you say, 'Fine, no problem! I'll just clean up after you!'"

Byron raised his eyebrows, not without resolve. "You have to trust me when I tell you this suicide was not unjustified. Not everything is evident to the naked eye."

Barnes shrugged her shoulders. *Whatever!* "Okay, tell me what happened when you found her body."

"Well, the plan was for me to go to her apartment this morning. She gave me a key to let myself in. When I saw the gunshot wound and her open eyes staring at me, I knew something had gone wrong. You see, I kept hearing the words Lisa had said to me. She said, 'It won't be gory.' When I asked her how she was going to do it, she said, 'It won't be gory.'"

Barnes shook her head. "Death is famous for its inconsistencies."

Byron mused over the aroma of his beer. The hops seemed to be leaping upward out of the glass. "I just don't understand what happened."

Barnes leaned forward. "You want to know what I think? I think somebody killed her and made it look like a suicide, which was very convenient since she was planning a suicide anyway."

Byron paused, lost in thought. "Unhappily, you may be right."

71

Barnes ran the fingertips of her right hand up and down the squat scotch glass. The ice in the glass made it pleasantly cool to the touch. "I think someone went to her apartment with the express purpose of killing her. If the intent was to burglarize, why shoot her? And why was nothing taken? Even the money in Lisa's purse—the money that was meant to go to you—was undisturbed. I think one thing was taken from that apartment, and that was the means for the *intended* suicide. It could have been pills, or maybe a serum of some kind, but the lab techs found no trace of anything like that."

Byron listened closely as Barnes displayed her craft. He felt some *pull*, within, as if he had just connected with something foreign. *Something's coming,* he thought.

After imbibing a hasty sip of scotch, Barnes continued. "Listen to this: On Monday afternoon, I got called into a case over by the Hopkins campus. A young Hopkins coed by the name of Hillary Miles was found dead in her apartment. The autopsy showed she was smothered to death with a pillow. No forced entry and nothing disturbed in the apartment. What's the kicker? She's five weeks pregnant." *Why the hell am I telling him this? Fuck if I know.*

"Now, as I'm investigating this case, I talk with the captain of the Hopkins Campus Police. It turns out he's investigating a burglary that took place last weekend in the chaplain's office. Some files belonging to students undergoing counseling were stolen."

Byron listened through the fog of white noise permeating the bar.

"Now guess who's receiving counseling at the chaplain's office?" A pregnant pause. "None other than Hillary Miles. Apparently, Hillary had some *personal* problems. Wouldn't you classify pregnancy out of wedlock to be a *personal* problem?"

Byron nodded in agreement.

"And, for the punch line to this sordid tale, guess who was counseling Hillary?" Before Byron had time to think, Barnes answered the question herself. "Lisa Browning."

The priest shook his head in disbelief.

"These two cases are related. I think the guy who got Miles pregnant is the one who shot Lisa. He's eliminating everybody who knows. I just hope the killing stops here."

Finishing off the pint of Wicked Ale, Byron leaned back on his barstool. "Well, I must admit things do seem to fit neatly in your little scenario. You got any suspects?"

"No. Not yet." The bar was noisy and raucous. Barnes felt as if she were in a wind tunnel. "Oh, I meant to tell you: I can't give you the money we found in Lisa's purse until the Evidence Control Unit is willing to release it."

Byron nodded. "I've made arrangements for the cremation. When will you release the body to me?"

"Soon."

The priest nodded his head and sat, momentarily, in silence. "The Hindus see the spiritual path to God to be one of *tapas. Tapas* is a Sanskrit word meaning *to burn.* Life is always burning us. That's the way it gets our attention. And when we're attentive to life, we learn its lessons. In this sense, we're all being cremated."

"Wouldn't you say burning a dead body is a bit different?"

"No, not at all."

28

Professor Elliot Peachwater sat quietly in the study of his palatial home on Greenway Drive. From his comfortable Chippendale wing chair, he proudly surveyed his collection of leather-bound literary classics (he kept his philosophical and theological texts in his office at the University), his priceless medieval liturgical paintings, the intricate detail of the room's rosewood architectural paneling, the eclectic black marble desk, the magnificent crystal chandelier overhead. Peachwater saw himself as a seasoned thoroughbred: full professor of theology at a prestigious university, respected author and lecturer, devoted husband and father, a paradigm of culture and sophistication. The fact was he could live no other way.

Turning the snifter of Remy Martin slowly in his hand, watching the cognac glaze the sides of the glass, he thought of Hillary Miles and felt a bittersweet quickening in his loins. He closed his eyes. In the warm and peaceful confines of his castle, he fell into a dreamless sleep.

29

When Linda Barnes arrived at the squad room on Thursday morning, the phone was already ringing.

"Barnes here."

"Christ, Barnes, do you always take this long to answer the phone?"

She immediately recognized the voice. "Only when I know it's you, Plitt."

"Look, I did some work on the Browning woman."

"That's what I like about you, Plitt, always respectful."

"That's my nature, Barnes. I'm everybody's best friend. Anyway, the head wound is not consistent with a self-inflicted injury. The trajectory of the bullet angles downward. She didn't kill herself."

"Believe it or not, Plitt, I came to that conclusion myself."

"Are you trying to hurt my feelings, Barnes? Are you telling me you don't need me anymore?"

Barnes took a deep breath. "I need you, Plitt. Can you give me the time of death?"

"I put it at about one a.m."

"One o'clock...okay...anything else?"

Plitt paused momentarily for effect. "Yeah, Barnes. I'm working late tonight in the lab. Thought you might like to join me for a nightcap with the stiffs."

Barnes couldn't stop herself from laughing. "No, Plitt, I don't think so. You see, I'm having an affair with a priest. I have my priorities."

"Oh, well, can't blame a guy for trying."

"Good-bye, Plitt." Staring at her desk, she felt numb all over. *I can't believe I said that.*

30

Captain Swenson swallowed the last bite of his turkey club sandwich and reached for a toothpick from the breast pocket of his bright yellow shirt. Leaning back in his chair, toothpick in mouth, he knew that the juicy case he had always dreamed of was here. Being a campus cop was boring, but at least it paid the bills. Now he tasted a little adrenaline.

Fingering his Rolodex and finding the number, he made his call. "Detective Barnes. Hey, this is Captain Swenson."

"Hi. What's up?" Barnes dropped two sugar cubes into her cup of piping hot coffee.

"Well, I've got some information for you."

"Great. Let me grab a pen. Okay, shoot."

"First, just so you'll know, there were four files stolen from the chaplain's office. The Miles kid and three others. I talked to all three students this morning. I don't see any relationship between these kids and the Miles girl. One of the kids was being counseled because his mother is dying of cancer. He's having a pretty tough time dealing with it. Another student is a freshman who's having trouble adjusting to living away from home. The third kid hates his roommate and wants to live off campus."

Barnes took a gulp of coffee and burned her bottom lip. "Did any of the students know Miles?"

"Nope. But I did talk to the girl she roomed with last year. I told her you would want to talk with her."

"Good. What's her name and number?" Barnes could feel a blister forming on the inner surface of her bottom lip.

"Her name is Megan Drew...555-9071. Also, she gave me the name of Miles' old boyfriend. He's at Hopkins too. His name is Jeff Danforth...555-1430."

"You're doing good, Swenson. Anybody else?"

"One more. I suggest you talk to Professor Elliot Peachwater...555-1600. He was Miles' advisor. I talked to him yesterday. He says he doesn't know anything, but I would still talk to him. Megan Drew said that Miles and Peachwater were friendly."

"Okay. Well, I'll get cracking."

"Detective Barnes...one more thing. I've hit a dead end on the chaplain's office burglary. I've got no leads. So I'm closing out the case. But I would like to help you on this murder case."

"I won't forget you, Swenson. If I need you, you'll hear from me."

"Thanks, Detective. You know, sometimes things get boring over here. I'm just looking for some action."

"Swenson, none of us is satisfied. I dream of being bored."

"Yeah. Life is that way. What you dream about doesn't happen."

31

Father Byron walked the footpath on the wooded hillside adjacent to his Monkton home. The chill in the air told him the winter would be harsh. A precursor, perhaps, of the duty that lay before him. Moving within the recesses of thought, where some say the seeds of morality may still be fertile, he pondered what he would say to the friends and family of Lisa Browning. The police had told the family of the necessity to investigate the death. Byron was left with the funeral service. He thought it best to come clean—to lay everything out as honestly and compassionately as possible. He knew he would be hit hard with criticism for his complicity, but it wouldn't be the first time he had been under fire. He knew he would survive.

As he walked back in the direction of the house, a presence engulfed him. The presence was self-illuminating: *Trust the movements of life; be my servant.* The priest heard these words resonate in the depths of his heart. Some might call this the voice of God.

32

Huddled in the cold darkness of the faculty parking lot, he carefully opened the trunk of his black Mercedes sedan, retrieved his toolbox, and removed a hammer, a Kemper clean-up tool, and a long, narrow Phillips-head screwdriver. He closed the toolbox and trunk without making a sound.

Hunched down below the hood line of the surrounding cars, he methodically crept through the lot until he found the vehicle he was looking for—the 1993 Miata. The car was located at the far end of the lot, away from the dispersed light filtering its way through the windows of the Hopkins Club. Breathing deeply, he hunched down close to the ground. His brain buzzed with a hot, uncontrollable anger that, to his fevered mind, was completely justified. After all, he was a lone visionary, a solitary seer of truth...*why not say it...an unrecognized genius!*

There, in the black of night, he methodically punctured the tires of the Miata with the hammer and clean-up tool. Then he drove the screwdriver through the puncture points and into the hard rubber with the glee of a madman. He pounded away on all four tires until his wrists and forearms ached. Then he scurried back to his own car and returned the tools to their rightful place. Straightening his black silk bow tie and buttoning his pristine white dinner jacket, he returned, unnoticed, to the festivities.

Elliot Peachwater's impulsive reaction to the proceedings of the JHU Faculty Awards Night gave testimony to a brain and moral fiber gone dangerously skittish. In the fall of each year, the JHU faculty convened in the Hopkins Club for an evening of gourmet food and fine liquor (cigars and pipes and European cigarettes were, at one time, staples of the affair, but with political and ecological correctness taking high profile more recently, the once great pleasure of smoking had been cast into suppression) for the express purpose of recognizing colleagues for their extraordinary academic accomplishments over the twelve prior months. At Hopkins, the prizes went to the writers—to those who published, in the eyes of academia, seminal works in their respective fields.

For Peachwater, the evening had been going along just fine. He was at the top of his form—mixing with the intelligentsia and sensing proudly, if not correctly, that the proper respect was being bestowed upon him. But what really put a spring in his step was the fact that he had a book up for prize consideration in the area of "Philosophy and Religion." His only competition in the field was from a young assistant professor of philosophy who had published what Peachwater considered a "minor" and somewhat far-fetched volume on the relationship between Nietzsche's Ubermensch and the Bodhisattva of Buddhism. Peachwater considered his own book, on the other hand, to be groundbreaking. He believed his work, entitled *The Deconstruction of God: A Meta-Dialogue with Augustine, Leibniz, Heidegger, and Derrida*, defined what it meant to live in the post-modern religious era. It would be an understatement to say he was hungry for the prize. So when the accolades went instead to Professor Kennedy for his *Nietzsche Meets The Buddha*, something snapped in Peachwater's psyche, and as the darkness within expanded, a primeval force uprooted him from his chair and drove him to the faculty parking lot gasping for air.

33

Linda Barnes was not on time arriving at the office of the Dean of Students. She had arranged through the dean to question Megan Drew and Jeff Danforth. Showing up twenty minutes late didn't help her persona. She had come to learn that when you're dealing with death, you're always late.

Standing in the hall outside the dean's office, she composed herself and then made her entrance. In the outer office, a secretary sat behind a sleek teak desk, busying herself with stacks of computer printouts. To her right, along the wall, sat a young man and woman. The man was tall and lanky and looked as if he would have trouble growing a beard. He wore jeans, a blue and green tattersall shirt, and a red and green striped necktie. It seemed to Barnes that the young man was not accustomed to neckties. She was happy nonetheless that he had put one on. It indicated, at the very least, that he thought this was something to be taken seriously.

The young woman beside him was attractive and well groomed. She had long, golden blond hair, large, blue eyes, and that nearly translucent pale skin that women covet and men admire. Clad in tight, black mohair sweater and forest green and maroon plaid skirt, she had the telltale look of sophistication waiting to mature. Barnes thought how odd it was that these two were probably Hillary Miles' closest friends. They looked as if they ran in very different circles; it also appeared as if they weren't enjoying each other's company.

Barnes extended her hand to the young woman. "Hi, I'm Detective Linda Barnes. I take it you're Megan Drew?" Megan nodded as she shook Barnes' hand. "And you're Jeff Danforth?"

"Yes," Danforth said, giving Barnes a cold-fish handshake that left her feeling slightly uncomfortable.

"Well, I'm glad both of you could make it. Who wants to go first?"

The two students glanced at each other quickly. "I guess I will," said Megan.

"Okay, good." Barnes turned to the secretary. "Is it okay to use the dean's office? She told me it would be all right."

"You sure can," the secretary said with an air of efficiency. "Go right through that door. It's the office on the right."

Barnes followed Megan Drew into Dean Smith's office and closed the door behind her. The office was spacious, with the dean's desk and books and PC equipment at one end of the room, and a sitting area with two black leather sofas and three gold, overstuffed chairs at the other. Large, framed posters of European cities adorned the walls.

"These chairs look comfortable," Barnes said as she gracefully placed herself in the warm confines of one of the cocoon-like gold chairs. Megan followed suit, her long, golden hair merging with the fabric of the upholstery.

Barnes saw the youth and beauty before her with bittersweet regret and longing. At age forty-two, she knew the blush was off the rose, never to return. She also knew that someone had truncated the life of a beautiful young woman—a pregnant one, no less. The young girl before her made it all the more real.

"Megan, I need to ask you some questions about Hillary Miles."

"I'm ready."

"Okay. First, did Hillary have any enemies? Anyone who might want to harm her?"

Megan shook her head. "I've been asking myself the same question. You see, Hillary pretty much stayed to herself. She didn't have much of a social life. I really can't think of anyone who would want to hurt her."

"You were her best friend...right?"

"Yes."

"Did you know she was pregnant?"

"Yes."

"Good. Did she tell you who the father was?"

"No. I couldn't believe she wouldn't tell me. She said it was absolutely essential that no one know."

"Do you have any ideas about who it might be?"

"Jeff Danforth used to be her boyfriend. But I don't think it was him. When Hillary broke the relationship off, it was over."

"When did she stop seeing him?"

"About a year ago. He kept hanging around...asking her to come back, but she'd really had enough of him."

"What do you mean by 'enough'? Was he violent or abusive?"

"No, no...nothing like that. He was just immature. I think Hillary had just had enough of college-age guys. They can be real assholes."

"Yeah, I know. And don't think they grow out of it, either."

Megan laughed. "I guess we share a common desperation when it comes to men."

"Yeah, I guess we do."

Megan chicly swept several strands of her beautiful blond hair away from her forehead with the long, elegant fingers of her right hand. "You know, I think she was seeing a married man."

Barnes raised her eyebrows with great anticipation. "Really? Why do you say that?"

"Well, why else would she refuse to tell me anything about him?"

Detective Linda Barnes smiled, as she felt her brain putting the pieces of the puzzle in order. "All right. Let's see what we can make of this. Hillary is bored with guys her own age...right? So she gets hooked up with some older guy...a married man who has a lot to lose if the affair is discovered. He tells Hillary the relationship must be absolutely secretive. And she buys this...so much so, she won't even confide in you. And then, when she gets pregnant, Prince Charming panics. Maybe she tells him she wants to keep the child...who knows?"

"Jesus," Megan said with a look of immediate illumination. "You know something...she *was* friendly with someone here at Hopkins...an older man...a professor."

"Professor Peachwater, by any chance?"

"How did you know?"

"Well, let's just say he's on my list of people to talk to. Tell me, what did she say about Peachwater?"

"Well, I knew she was friends with him. A lot of students will hang

85

around professors that they really like. So I never thought anything about it. But now when I look back on it, something may have been going on there. I know she was very impressed with his intelligence...he was her advisor...and I guess when she went to him for advice on which classes to take, they would start to talk about philosophy and religion...things that Hillary really found interesting. Anyway, I know she was smitten with him."

"Well, I'll be interested in talking to Peachwater. Look, another question...do you know Lisa Browning?"

Megan thought for a moment. "I don't think so. Why?"

"No particular reason. Tell me, did Hillary ever tell you she was seeing a shrink or counselor...anything like that?"

"No. Was she?"

"I don't think it matters. One other thing, do you know the name of Hillary's gynecologist?"

Megan shook her head. "She told me that she went to some walk-in clinic for her diaphragm. It's strange when you think about it. A classy girl like Hillary going to some clinic like that."

"Do you know which clinic she went to?"

"No. She never told me."

Barnes stared at the girl for a moment, lost in some intuitive dimension. "Thanks, Megan. You've been a great help."

"That's okay, Detective. I needed to talk about her. Hillary didn't have many close buddies. So I really haven't had the chance to talk to anyone who really knew her."

"I'm sorry you lost your friend, Megan."

"I'm sorry too."

34

Elliot Peachwater stuck his large, handsome head through the office doorway. "Roger? You busy?"

Roger Kennedy looked up from the book he was reading. "Oh, hi, Elliot. How are things with you today?"

"Can't complain, Roger. Look, I heard about the vandalism to your car. It's horrible to think that that kind of thing can happen right here on campus."

Kennedy seemed resolved to dismiss the whole matter. "What can I say? It happens."

Peachwater could feel his mind starting to spin off its axis. "Do you ever think that sometimes these apparently random events are justified? Or, in some way, deserved?"

Kennedy was silent, surprised by Peachwater's line of thought. "Well, I suppose some would chalk it up to karma."

"I'm not talking about *karma*," Peachwater said harshly. "I'm talking about *real justice*. I'm talking about a wrong being set right. I'm talking about greatness being recognized and mediocrity assuming its own level."

Kennedy had always been uncomfortable around Peachwater, and now was no exception. "Elliot, I'm not sure what you're getting at."

"Well, then you'll have to improve your listening skills, Roger." Peachwater's voice was loud and piercing. "Anyone with half a mind *knows* that I should have won the prize in 'Philosophy and Religion.' And maybe this little event in the parking lot is especially meaningful in that it symbolically delivers that message. Not that anyone else has understood this but me. Sometimes I really believe that I'm the only one that *sees*, the only one that *knows* what's happening."

Kennedy sat at his desk in a state of complete entropy. It was as if he had been shot with a stun gun. As his mind cleared, he saw for the first time that Peachwater was mad. A true egomaniac, a sociopath. "Elliot, I really don't know what to say. I don't think anyone was trying to discredit your book."

"Oh, Christ! What do you know? The so-called scholars at this University imagine they know what real thinking is. Well, they don't! They just don't have the gift. The muse of wisdom and insight doesn't visit them. They have no idea what true genius is!"

The room fell silent.

"Well, do *you* understand, Roger? Or do I have to explain it to you again?"

"I understand."

"Good. I think it's so important that human beings *genuinely* communicate."

Kennedy didn't move a muscle. He just wanted to be rid of this dark presence.

Peachwater smiled with a relieved sense of satisfaction. "Well, I feel much better now that we've cleared the air. I've got to go. I have some students coming around. Good-bye, Roger."

"Good-bye, Elliot."

Roger Kennedy got up slowly from his desk and closed the door to his office. Walking carefully, as if he had just been in some kind of car wreck, he went to the office window and stared out onto the quadrangle below. He took a deep breath and then felt a subterranean shaking within—a shaking that he let run its course into uncontrollable laughter. What was so funny—*curious* funny, not *ha, ha* funny—was the *finality* of it all, the *certainty* of it all. To see madness standing before you in the bright light of day carries a heavy satisfaction. It's rare to ever see anything in life that clearly, and when it happens, time simply stops at the measure of certitude. It was only later, upon reflection, that Kennedy recognized the bitter side of this realization: there is such a thin, precarious line between madness and genius, between self-delusion and understanding. What is it that tips the balance one way or the other? Who would pretend to know?

35

Julie Trabor was nineteen years old. She had a pinup body and long, coal black hair that reached just below her waist. She was smart. Sexy smart. Street smart. Dangerous smart.

"So what do you think? Should I take your class next semester?"

Peachwater smiled as he shifted anticipatorily in his chair. "I think it would do you good. Expand your mind. Give you a break from physics and chemistry."

Julie flashed a sarcastic smile. "I've never taken an upper-level theology course. Do you think I'll pass?"

"Tillich's Systematic Theology isn't easy. But perhaps with a little tutoring..." Peachwater stopped speaking and gazed at the hormone-popping vixen before him with a peculiar faraway look that spoke of fantasy and longing.

Julie Trabor purred, "Well, if you promise to help me, I'll take your class."

"I promise, Julie. I promise."

Julie Trabor got out of her chair, walked slowly across the room, and locked the door to Peachwater's office. She then turned and made her way back to where the professor sat behind his desk. Dressed in a short, tight, black leather skirt and a revealing V-neck, white lamb's wool sweater, she slid up onto Peachwater's desk and dangled her shapely legs before him.

Peachwater caught her eyes with his and slowly slid his right hand up her skirt. As her legs parted ever so slightly, the phone *rang*...and *rang* again. Neither of them so much as budged. Then, eyes still melded together, hand still moving up her thigh, Peachwater lifted the phone with his left hand and brought it to his ear.

"Peachwater here."

"Professor Peachwater, this is Detective Linda Barnes with the Baltimore City Police Department."

Peachwater continued to caress the coed with eyes and hand. "Well, Detective, what can I do for you?"

"I'd like to make an appointment with you to talk about Hillary Miles. I assume you're aware of her death."

"Yes. I was very sorry to hear about it." Peachwater could feel wet sex on his fingers through the girl's panties.

"Would ten on Monday morning be good for you?"

"Give me one minute to check my calendar," Peachwater said with trumped-up concern in his voice. He closed his eyes and pressed the phone to his chest. The girl was beginning to moan, and Peachwater's fingers felt the jazzy electric current she gave off.

"Shhhh...," he said softly to the orgasmic one, while bringing the phone back to his ear. "Yes, Detective, ten on Monday would be fine."

"At your office. Okay?"

"Right. See you at ten."

The black-haired vixen slid off the desk and stood before Peachwater with her hands on her shapely hips. "How old are you, Professor?"

"Forty-seven, my love."

"You're older than my father."

Peachwater smiled. "You're younger than my daughter."

36

Tom Percy, clad in lime green T-shirt and multicolored tattersall Bermuda shorts, sat wearily on the edge of his cot. He looked at his watch: 6:00 a.m. Sri Peche would already be at the river. The devotees as well. He slipped into his sandals and cap, grabbed his knapsack, and set off.

The blazing sun, beginning to crest on the mountain ridge, seared the horizon like a hot poker. Percy walked along a dirt path gradually descending to the river Cavery. To the west, he saw rice paddies worked by oxen and a few brown men in white dhotis. To the east were the vegetable gardens—colorful and vibrant in the early morning hours. After ten minutes of steady walking, he entered a thicket of dense woods. He heard the faint chanting of mantrams below him in the distance.

The thicket was cool and damp, a pleasant contrast to the oppressive heat of India. Soon, the thatched roof of nature opened to occasional shafts of sunlight, and finally he emerged into the open air of mystical enchantment: the sacred river Cavery; the crowd of disciples chanting mantrams in unison; the cool, thick mist hovering above the river; and the man they all came to worship—Sri Peche.

Percy made his way down the narrow beach, thick with worshipers trying to catch a glimpse of Sri Peche. Materially, these people had nothing to speak of. Life at Bodhichitta Hermitage was like stepping back into the Middle Ages. To be with Sri Peche was all they wanted, all they needed. The followers' countenances spoke this truth. Many of the faces were toothless, some were missing eyes, some were drawn to contortion by stroke. But they all gleamed with happiness—a happiness rooted deep within their hearts.

When he reached the river's edge, Percy saw Sri Peche bathing in the sacred waters. Watching him wash his hair, face, beard, and frail body, he felt as if he were witnessing some aboriginal ballet—the movements crisp yet flowing, mundane yet majestic.

When Sri Peche emerged from the river wearing nothing but a white dhoti, the devotees bowed before him, reaching out to touch the tops of his feet and ankles as he walked by. Sri Peche, in turn, gently touched their heads or shoulders as he passed through the crowd. Two young women, carrying towels and sarong, came forward to meet him. After drying off and wrapping the sarong around his waist, Sri Peche initiated the procession back to Bodhichitta Hermitage. He walked slowly and rhythmically across the beach, through the thicket, and up the dirt road to the clay porch outside his hut. The devotees followed him, chanting mantrams, with heads bowed.

Sri Peche sat in a wicker chair on the porch. The sunlight, reflecting off his white hair and beard, danced like a thousand crystals floating in the air. His disciples sat around him on cloth mats. Some lucky ones were close by on the porch, the rest on the ground. Percy watched and listened carefully as they posed questions and Sri Peche answered them. Some of the questions were asked and answered in Tamil, others in English. Sometimes Sri Peche answered in silence— the kind of silence that explodes and rumbles deep within. After about thirty minutes, the guru gave a communal blessing, and everyone dispersed. Two young women escorted Sri Peche inside the hut.

Tom Percy waited patiently at the edge of the porch. Finally, an attendant came out and beckoned him to enter the hut. As Percy pushed through the beads hanging over the thatched threshold, he felt a distinct auditory explosion within, as if he had broken through some metaphysical sound barrier. For a moment, the interior thunder blurred his vision and affected his balance, but soon his inner ear repressurized.

Sri Peche reclined on a thin mattress on the floor, his torso raised up comfortably with pillows. He told his attendants to leave and asked Percy to sit in the wooden chair next to the mattress.

Sri Peche smiled. "I guess you'll want to tape the interview."

Percy raised his eyebrows as he pulled the tape recorder out of his knapsack. "Yes, if you don't mind."

"It doesn't matter to me. What periodical are you writing for?"

Percy placed the recorder on the mattress and turned it on. "I'm with the *Village Voice*. It's based in New York City."

"Hmmm."

"Forgive me, Sri Peche. I haven't introduced myself. My name is Tom Percy."

Sri Peche nodded. "New York City. It's been many years since I walked *those* crowded streets."

Percy took off his cap and, not knowing where to put it, placed it on the dirt floor. "What you find in New York is far removed from what you find here—that's for sure."

"Oh, it's really the same everywhere. People are just people. Wherever you find them."

Lying on the mattress, covered only by a white dhoti, Sri Peche looked like a frail scarecrow. His skin hung on his bones like loose fabric. Yet behind those black, recessed eyes was the power of a purposeful lion. Percy, sensing this in every cell of his body, felt his mouth go dry.

The words from Sri Peche shattered the silence: "Mr. Percy, why are you here? What is it you want to know?"

Sri Peche's eyes were like black, bottomless pools. Percy struggled to find his voice. "Sri Peche, I must be honest with you. My reason for being here is to reveal to the world who you really are."

Sri Peche breathed with sustained stillness. "Go on. It's okay."

"I know about the legends—that you're considered a saint, that miracles have issued from you, that you are an instrument of God. I also know that your past has been shrouded in mystery. You don't speak of it, and there isn't much of a trail to link you to it." Percy waited for Sri Peche to respond, but only silence filled the hut.

Percy got up from the chair and walked to the end of the mattress. For some reason, sitting close to Sri Peche was unnerving. "I've been tracking down the facts of your life for over four years, off and on. I know that you are close to eighty years old, that you were born in London, that you were raised in Chicago; that you attended Northwestern Theological Seminary and became an Episcopal priest. I know that you married into a wealthy family, that you fathered a son. I know you are Alexander Peachwater."

Sri Peche's eyes twinkled. "Very true. It's all very true."

"I'm going to put it all in my story about you."

Sri Peche smiled and took a deep breath. "It's okay. I don't mind. My life is an open book. Print what you know to be true. But always remember: you can never know the *whole* story. No one can. Not even me." Sri Peche paused, turned the palms of his hands up, and gazed at them as if he were reviewing old photographs he had not seen for years. "We are not entirely transparent—even to ourselves."

For the next ten minutes, Percy told Sri Peche all he knew about him, and Sri Peche confirmed it. As the interview went on, Percy could feel the *presence* of the guru before him—a presence not unlike the pregnant stillness before a storm.

"Sri Peche, what I don't know is what motivated you to do what you have done. What motivated you to leave your parish and your family? And why go to India? Why all the secrecy?"

Sri Peche smiled. "Very good questions." Sri Peche waved his hand gracefully, beckoning Percy to come closer. Percy sat on the chair and leaned down to listen. Sri Peche placed the fingertips of his right hand on Percy's forehead and whispered into his ear, "I will answer your questions tomorrow. You will be ready to hear the truth at that time."

Percy's head jerked backward involuntarily. He grabbed his knees in a fit of dizziness. Breathing deeply, he sat quietly until he regained his equilibrium. When he looked up, Sri Peche was moving through the doorway out to the patio. Percy got up but was struck again with dizziness. He sat down and closed his eyes.

When he woke, he could hear the laughter of children outside the hut. Moving through the doorway, he was surprised to discover that it was dusk. The children had eaten their supper and were enjoying the last moments of play before bedtime. Percy was not hungry, just exhausted. He walked back to his hut and fell into a deep sleep.

The bright white light hurt his eyes, but he couldn't look away. Finally, the light softened, and he saw Sri Peche sitting in a bamboo chair. Sri Peche beckoned him to come close. "Sit at my feet." Percy did so. Sri Peche leaned down and placed his hand on Percy's shoulder. "Truth is power. You have to be careful with it. If you want the whole truth, the price you pay is your own silence. When you really know what's going on, you do whatever is necessary, whatever you are called upon to do. The drama of life must be allowed to unfold. Sometimes your role is to speak the truth; at other times you are to remain silent. When you know the whole truth, you will be made to speak or not to speak by a higher power. When you live this way, you are a pure instrument of God."

37

Percy opened his eyes. His body felt heavy, like a barbell one dreads to lift. He was surprised to find he had slept in his clothes. He looked at his watch: 10:30 a.m. *My God, the interview!* He rolled off the cot and stood up. His mouth felt dry and grassy. He sipped some water from his canteen, grabbed his knapsack, and headed off in the direction of Sri Peche's hut.

The sun burned high in the sky and was unusually bright. When he arrived at Sri Peche's hut, no one was about. He walked across the porch, pulled back the beads that hung in the doorway, and looked inside. Sri Peche was on his mattress, propped up by pillows, writing in a notebook.

Sri Peche looked up and smiled. "Mr. Percy, I've been expecting you."

Percy entered the hut. "Forgive me, Sri Peche. I know you make time for interviews after your morning bath. I overslept. I can't understand it. I never sleep past six. I hope you can speak with me now."

Sri Peche smiled calmly. "As I said, I've been expecting you."

Percy prepared the tape recorder and placed it on the mattress next to Sri Peche. He pressed the RECORD button. "Sri Peche, I'd like to pick up where we left off yesterday." Percy pulled the wooden chair next to the mattress and sat down. He took a deep breath and shook his head. "I don't know what's happening to me. I'm feeling dizzy again." He took another deep breath. "To tell you the truth, I don't remember where we left off yesterday. When I got up to leave your hut, you were gone. And then, I went straight to bed. I must have slept over twelve hours."

Sri Peche nodded and pointed to the other side of the hut. "There's a pitcher of mango juice on my desk. Pour yourself a cup and drink it. You'll feel better."

Percy walked to the desk and poured himself a cup of juice. "Can I get some for you?"

"No, I'm fine."

Percy drank the juice and returned to his seat. For several minutes he sat quietly in some refined contemplation. Then, surprising himself, he leaned forward and turned off the tape recorder. "Tell me the truth about yourself. I won't print anything you tell me today. I just want to know."

Sri Peche smiled. "Very well. In my mid thirties, I was enjoying my duties as an Episcopal priest in Cambridge, Massachusetts. I served in a well-to-do parish and led a very pleasant, if uneventful, life. Although I was not touched deeply by the presence of God, I felt that nothing was lacking."

Sri Peche paused, a mischievous twinkle in his eyes. "Then, everything changed. A divorcee entered the parish. She was like no woman I had ever seen, and something about her overwhelmed me. To make a long story short, she seduced me. There was no love in this scenario. Just a craziness of longing and lust—and *fear*. I knew to be fearful but didn't listen to myself. To be honest, she had more power than I did. I had some sense of God, but what she had was more powerful."

Sri Peche looked at Percy with eyes that had seen the other shore. "She had the devil in her. I say this in all seriousness."

Sri Peche straightened the pillows behind him. "Well, not long after we commenced the affair, she became pregnant. I did what any

101

respectable man would do—I married her. I knew she was evil. I knew she was crazy. But I did what I thought was right. Nine months later, my son was born. The moment I saw him, I knew there was more of her than me in him—much more. I knew that I, a man of God, had participated in giving birth to the devil—or, I should say, an instrument of the devil. I need not tell you about the despair that poisoned my heart."

Sri Peche raised his right hand, index finger pointing upward. "But then something changed in me. I felt as if my personality and everything I had previously identified with had been sucked out of me. I saw my body as some shell-like apparatus, and within the shell was nothing—just emptiness. The emptiness was as sweet as nectar, as vast and free as the infinity of space, as peaceful and poignant as a constant flame on a windless night. And, most important, there was a wisdom, a compassion that was absolutely clarifying."

Percy sat spellbound, shaking his head in perplexity. "Sri Peche, I'm not doubting the veracity of what you say. It's just that I don't understand such things."

Sri Peche smiled. "Oh, believe me, I didn't understand myself. Not until I experienced the presence of God within me. Then it became clear."

A gradual smile came over Percy's face. "Well, don't keep me in suspense."

Sri Peche sat straight up and leaned toward his friend. "The first thing to understand is this: the life that we experience through our senses and contemplate with our mind is nothing other than God. But it is not God in its transcendent state. It is God in its manifest state. In its transcendent state, God is the one unified source of all that is. Whatever shows up here in this world comes from that source.

"In its manifest state, however, it appears as multiplicity. This is what is so confusing. Within our world of space and time, God expresses itself as diversity in ever-increasing increments of complexity. What we take to be differences, however, comprise a special-effects show produced by God. That's what we need to remember. What we see here is the special-effects show, not the truth that lies behind it.

"In its transcendent state, God is pure possibility. God is *one* unified source of pure potentiality. Anything can come out of this pure potency—anything! It is the manifestation of the infinity of possibilities that we see as the phenomenal world. If you really understand this, you see that statements like 'God is good' or 'God is love' are only pieces of the truth. The fact is God is also evil, God is also hatred. Everything in this world is an expression of God! So, from this point of view, it is no mystery that I could give birth to a devil. God was using me to bring forth another expression of its possibilities."

Sri Peche gently placed his hand on Percy's arm. "Tom, the key to all of it is acceptance, unconditional acceptance. Whatever life brings, accept it. Whatever life takes away, accept that also. If you don't like what's happening, and you feel moved to change it, do whatever you think is right. But then again, accept the results of your actions. Know that whatever happens is simply God's special-effects show. You have a part in the show. All you have to do is play your part. God will make you do what is necessary."

Sri Peche smiled mischievously. "From the moment this understanding dawned within me, I have been truly happy. And from that moment on, I have seen my destiny."

The heat from Sri Peche's hand soothed Percy's arm. "Sri Peche, what did you do about your marriage?"

"I stayed. I weathered the storm of evil and insanity. It was my destiny to do so. And when my son turned eighteen, I disappeared. That too was my destiny. I assure you, none of this was my plan. It is all God's plan."

"Do you ever wonder about your son?"

"There is nothing to wonder about. I know what he is."

"I'm not so sure you do. Do you realize that he's turned out quite well? He's a highly respected member of the intelligentsia in the States."

Sri Peche looked at Percy with sad realization. "Remember what I said about the diversity of God. I have no doubt about my son's intelligence. The question is what is in his heart? I know what is there. It is not pretty."

Percy shook his head. "I don't know what to say. This is quite a story."

"Is it a story you feel compelled to share with the world?"

Percy laughed nervously. "No, I don't think so. It's nobody's business but yours."

Sri Peche smiled. "It's all God's business."

38

Linda Barnes did a balancing act with her groceries as she unlocked the door to her apartment. A pale light filtered through the living room window from the streetlamps below. Navigating her way into the kitchen, she flicked on the switch for the overhead light with her elbow and slid the bags onto the butcher-block table. From where she stood, she could see the answering machine in the dining room flashing *red*.

Christ, I hope that's not important.

She unpacked her groceries, kicked off her shoes, cracked open a brand new bottle of fifteen-year-old Singleton single malt scotch, poured about three fingers, neat, into a glass, and settled down on the shirr-skirted, country chaise in the living room. She sat there in the dark, sipping the Singleton, thoughts moving in and out of mental focus.

I'm slipping away. I'm really slipping away. For the first time in my life, I'm afraid of who I am.

She took a deep breath. As she exhaled, she heard an alien cry echoing inside her. A cry of loneliness, insidious self-doubt, longing. *Something else as well. Not clearly identifiable. A bitter taste in her mouth. Tastes like dissonance. Tastes like evil.* She swung herself around, feet hitting the floor. Her neck and spine slowly gave way as her head descended between her knees, tongue hanging loose in her dry mouth, tears cascading down the bridge of her nose. In this strange catatonia, she remained frozen indefinitely.

Layers upon layers of blackness, darkness. An absence of light infused throughout. Somewhere in the blackness she hears shrill, insidious laughter. Laughter that could provoke one to spin off one's axis. Now she is swimming up through the thick sea of darkness, wanting to surface, but bringing the darkness with her.

She woke with a start. Her eyes burned, and her head felt as if it were floating. The empty scotch glass lay on its side on the hardwood floor. Placing the glass upright, she got up and steadied herself. Walking gingerly toward the flashing red light, she imagined it was a sign, a beacon directing her to an answer to all her questions and doubts. She pushed the PLAY button and listened. "Linda, this is Dick Byron." There was a long pause. "I was wondering if you might want to join me for a drink tonight. I'll be at the Manor Tavern."

39

The priest looked at his watch: 11:00 p.m. *She's not coming,* he thought. He had looked at his watch, in just this fashion, three times this evening; and each time he told himself she wasn't coming, and each time he ordered another Bass Ale and refused to leave. *It's funny,* he thought, *I couldn't leave here if I wanted to. Somehow it's necessary that I stay and wait.* He smiled and laughed to himself. *I'm just a puppet. The movements of life pull the strings.* He was breathing heavily now. The alcohol was taking its toll. He could feel his mind beginning to numb. It was not a deleterious numbing, but rather a rarefied philosophical numbing, that was not without clarity, that caused no fear of thinking the truth.

Dick Byron sensed a body nearby and saw a hand wrap itself around the back of the chair next to him.

"Hi, Dick. You're drinking too much again."

Byron looked up and saw her face as if it were a Madonna under light.

"Linda...you came."

"I'm here, Dick. I'm sorry I'm so late. It's been a difficult day."

"I know. You want a drink?"

Barnes slipped into the chair next to him. "Not now." She leaned forward in confidence. "Dick, I had a real scare tonight."

"What happened?" Byron asked, obviously concerned.

Barnes swept a fingertip across her left eyelid. Byron saw she had been crying. "I think I experienced a 'dark night of the soul.'"

Byron stroked his short-cropped beard. "Welcome to the club."

Barnes stared at the table, lost in inwardness. "It was very eerie. I felt like I was losing myself to madness. There was no hope at all in that place, no resolution. And then, I just checked out. I really mean it. I was just gone. I'm not sure, but I think hours passed by."

"Are you okay now?"

"Yeah, I am. Hearing your voice on the answering machine brought me back to the living."

Byron smiled. "Well, I'm here to serve."

Barnes laughed and shook her head. "Yeah? Well, how about letting me use you as a sounding board?"

"You're all work, aren't you?" Byron stared at the inviting notch of her neck. A hint of perspiration glistened there.

Barnes pursed her lips together. "This morning I questioned Hillary Miles' ex-roommate and ex-boyfriend. The boyfriend didn't know anything. Hillary jilted him a year ago. He tried to stay in her life, but she wasn't interested."

"Affairs of the heart. They can be messy."

Barnes smirked. "Her ex-roommate, though, was another story. You see, women who are tight with each other share *everything*. But this was a situation where Hillary wasn't talking. Whoever she was involved with could not afford any leaks."

Byron nodded. The notch of Linda Barnes' neck was still of great interest to him.

"Now listen to this. The ex-roommate said that Hillary had had enough of immature guys, and she had the feeling that Hillary may have been seeing an older, married man. Well, this isn't exactly extraordinary, right? So why won't Hillary talk about it to her best friend? I think it's because this guy has forbidden her to do so. He cannot be found out. He'll even kill to prevent it."

Byron sipped the Bass Ale with reverence. "Do you have any leads?"

"Nothing concrete. But there is a professor she was fond of. In fact, the roommate said Hillary was smitten with him. Actually, this guy is in your field—so to speak."

"What do you mean?"

"He's a professor of theology. His name is Peachwater."

Byron's eyes opened wide. "Peachwater! I'll be damned."

"What do you mean?" Barnes asked with an expression of confusion.

"Well...I know him."

"You know him?" Barnes asked.

"Yeah, I *know* Elliot Peachwater. We taught together at Georgetown. Must have been ten to twelve years ago."

Barnes was silent. She couldn't believe what she was hearing. "God, Dick, this is just too strange. All these lives intersecting."

Byron smiled. "It's really not so strange. All our lives intersect all the time. We're just not aware of it."

Barnes felt stirring within her an attraction to this strange and inscrutable man. She very much wanted to get on with other things, but the habit of being a cop always on the job continued to persist. "What's Peachwater like? Do you think he could be our man?"

"I haven't been around him in a long time. So I really couldn't say." Byron paused in some decisive, pondering stare, running a hand through his disheveled hair. "I don't like judging people as a rule. But I guess, in this instance, I should tell you what I've observed."

Barnes stared at Byron, nonplussed. "Yes, Dick, you *should* tell me."

"Peachwater and I didn't get on well together. He has a pathological need to be the focus of attention. He didn't fancy the idea of anyone else in the department receiving any praise. But what was really eerie was his apparent delight in hurting others—or, perhaps, it was just that he didn't care who got hurt as long as he got what he wanted. And, yes—anticipating your question—he did hit on the coeds."

Barnes sat spellbound. "Tell me more."

"Peachwater has led a privileged life. He comes from old Eastern Shore money. Ph.D. from the School of Divinity at Yale. Married a society girl. Fathered a daughter. And he has authored a few respectable books. He lives well."

"I can't wait to catch his act tomorrow," Barnes said, shaking her head with a mixture of disgust and pointed anticipation.

Byron's face became serious. "All in all, I would classify him as a dangerous man. Be careful."

Barnes raised her eyebrows. "Do you think he's capable of murder?"

Byron stroked his bearded chin. "Linda, these kinds of things are beyond speculation. I think none of us knows our capacity for doing good *or* evil. Sometimes life bears down on us, and we end up doing things we could never imagine. I'm sure there are times when people literally no longer recognize themselves. The problem is we have to find ways to live with the consequences of what we do."

Barnes stared at the priest. "You didn't answer my question. Do you think Peachwater is capable of murder?"

Byron took a deep breath. "Yes, I do. There is an evil presence about him. Believe me when I tell you that kind of presence is rare."

Barnes' lips formed a sardonic smile. "With that pronouncement, I think I'll have a well-deserved drink." Barnes scratched the top of her left ear. *Tender to the touch. And pointy. Odd.*

Barnes. Walking to the bar. Pointy ear burning ever so slightly. Flagging down the bartender. "I'll have a double Glenlivet. No rocks."

Barnes. Eavesdropping on the lovey-dovey couple sitting next to her at the bar. Musing, *This young bitch is sticky with infatuation. In a year, she'll want to kick his face in.*

"Excuse me, but that'll be nine dollars," the bartender said.

Barnes. Coming back from her uncomfortable reverie. Not liking where she's been. Pointy ear burning. "Oh, here's ten. Keep it."

Linda Barnes walked slowly back to her table. *What's happening to me?*

Byron looked up at her. "Are you okay? You look like you've seen a ghost."

Barnes shrugged her shoulders. "Maybe I'm coming down with something. Whatever." She sat down and leaned forward. "And what about you, Dick? How are things with you?"

"Me? I just keep rolling along. I just do my part in the big drama."

Linda laughed. *Is that true contentment I see in his eyes?* "The big drama. Is that what this is?"

"Yeah, I think so," Byron said matter-of-factly. "Life is an unfolding dramatic event. And everything on earth is playing a part. I just try to be attentive to what the director wants me to do. Life speaks in many voices. The key is to learn how to listen."

"What do you mean by 'listen'?"

"Well, real listening can't take place unless one is quiet inside. The big drama is not about us as individuals. It's about the totality of the cosmos."

Linda looked at the priest, communicating silently for him to continue.

"If we can clear away our own personal, egocentric drama, we can see the larger drama of life in totality—how everything is connected to everything else—how every person's singular life is just a facet or aspect of life in totality. People are really not separate from one another. We are interrelated parts of a single, magnificent event that is life itself. But we never can see or understand this as long as we're caught within our limited, egocentric perspective. In fact, it's only when we let go of all our ideas of a personal self that life truly opens up to us. The problem is that we don't want to give up the ego. It's too scary—we think we'll die."

Linda stared at the priest, her eyes glassing over. "Jesus, Dick. I don't know what to say. I had trouble with Philosophy 101."

The priest smiled. "Ah, I'm talking too much. What is, is; what is not, is not."

Linda stared at Byron with growing fondness. "Do you consider yourself a good priest?"

Byron looked at her, not knowing what to say. "Linda, I'm a priest only in name. I have not believed in the dogma of the Catholic Church for a long time. In fact, I don't even have a parish. It may sound strange, but I don't identify myself as anyone anymore. I'm just here in the stream of life. I trust life's intelligence, its wisdom, its energy. I myself have no need for some personal intelligence or wisdom. I'm here at the service of life. It moves me about. It makes all the choices."

"Is life just another word for God?"

"If you wish. It's just a word to signify the intelligence, the energy that makes things happen."

"Dick, can I ask you something personal?" Something in her voice spoke of urgency. "Where do I fit into all this?" Byron stared at her but said nothing. "Cop meets priest. What does life say about that?"

Byron tilted his pint of Bass Ale to the side and watched the libation coat the glass with amber swirls. "For some reason, life has brought us together. Who knows why? I recognize that I'm drawn to you. This is not something I choose."

The two sat in silence.

Barnes shook her head. "Don't you want to know how I feel?"

"I know how you feel. The magnet is not pulling just one of us."

40

Father Byron climbed the wooded Monkton hillside without much difficulty. The sun, gently floating on the horizon, illuminated his path with shards of gold and orange light. Each time his walking stick struck the nearly frozen ground, an echo of mortality rang out to the universe. A few hear these echoes all the time—others are not quiet enough to hear.

Byron used these neighboring hillsides in the same way that Nietzsche used the mountain paths of Sils Maria. Walking, climbing, dwelling—all to clear the mind in order to *listen*, in order to *hear* what life was saying.

Stopping to rest, Byron perched himself comfortably on a large rock and surveyed the valley below. He was fifty-three years old, twenty-five years away from the seminary and what seemed a lifetime away from what he used to believe as a Catholic priest. He still wore the collar when necessary and performed ceremonial duties when called upon to do so by the occasional unsuspecting believer. All in all, an innocent sham. Not without purpose.

Father Byron felt a warm tingle spiral up his spine. His eyes closed, and his breathing became deep and slow. *He could see it coming now in his mind's eye. A dark, cold presence. A presence carrying the blinding dust of mayhem on its wings. Anything can happen,* he thought. *The unexpected is no stranger.*

The priest shifted slightly on the rock in order to brace himself against a strong gust of wind that seemed to come out of nowhere. Then, looking up into the eye of the cool, orange sun through the nearly bare branches of the tall tulip poplars, he observed his attention catch and hold fast to a single leaf, torn lose by the wind, cascading down in a free-fall ballet toward the earth. The leaf reminded him of something Swami Satchidananda said in *The Master's Touch*. Seeing a single leaf caught in a swirl of water and swept over a dam, Swamiji said, *Enlightenment is this way. Suddenly, one breaks free.*

Looking at his watch, he saw it was time to begin the journey back home. There was much to be done. This morning he would view the cremation of Lisa Browning's body and prepare the urn. Then he would meet with the Hopkins chaplain to oversee preparation of the Garrett Room at the University, where the memorial service would take place tomorrow. Tonight, he would think about what he would say at the service and to the family of the deceased. Time waits for no one.

41

When Detective Linda Barnes arrived at Professor Peachwater's office at ten o'clock Monday morning, she found a handwritten note taped to the open door:

> Detective Barnes,
>
> Make yourself at home; have gone to get coffee and pastries.
>
> E.P.

Half-surprised at Peachwater's thoughtfulness, Barnes removed the note from the door and placed it in her blazer pocket. Retaining the note was a habitual reflex of being a cop. You never knew when something apparently insignificant might suddenly become valuable to cracking a case. *On second thought,* Barnes mused, *this note is pure bullshit.* She retrieved it from her pocket, crumpled it up, and tossed it into a shiny black wastebasket, embossed with the gold Hopkins shield, conveniently located by Peachwater's over-sized teak desk.

So this is Peachwater's home away from home, Barnes said silently to herself. Peachwater's office was anything but modest. The parquet floor was adorned with Persian rugs; an expansive Chinese tapestry hung on one wall, accentuating the grand, twelve-foot ceiling. Another wall encased windows through which warm sunlight saturated the room and danced on the rich colors of the rugs and silken scroll. The remaining two walls displayed Peachwater's ostentatious library.

Making her way along the rows and rows of books, Detective Barnes surveyed Peachwater's monument to himself. The texts were arranged in alphabetical order by author: Aquinas, Aristotle, Augustine,

Descartes, Diderot, Freud, Goethe, Hegel, Heidegger, James, Jaspers, Kant, Kierkegaard, Lenin, Marx, Nietzsche, Otto. On and on, the brain-foggers continued, unfolding overly complex visions of what might be.

Barnes stopped when she came to the section where Peachwater had his own writings displayed: *The Deconstruction of God* had joined *Religion in a World Come of Age, Ethics in an Age of Conflict,* and *Vestiges of the Sacred* already ensconced on the shelf. She pulled out the book on ethics and read the short foreword:

The word "ethics" is derived from the Greek ethos, meaning *character*—and in the plural, *manners*. Hence, ethical activity always refers to and says something about one's character, about the ways one relates to others, about the manners one expresses in conducting one's affairs. Ethical situations and dilemmas will test and, in some sense, measure the depths of one's character or, as Kierkegaard would say, the state of one's "inwardness." When Socrates says "Know thyself," he is talking about one's inwardness, the ethical self. He is talking about knowing what virtue is in both thought and deed.

It is the author's sincere wish that this humble book may help to illuminate what value *goodness* may yet hold in a world threatened by both internal and external conflict.

Elliot Peachwater
October 1985
JHU

Peachwater whispered in Barnes' ear, "Did you find something interesting?"

Barnes' heart jumped. A slow, spiraling chill rose up her spine. "Professor Peachwater, I presume?" she said without turning around.

"That's *riiight*," Peachwater said with the slightest touch of sarcasm in his voice. "And you must be Detective Barnes."

Barnes turned around and faced Peachwater squarely. "That's *riiight.*"

Peachwater, not liking the way she had turned the tables on him, smiled halfheartedly, walked over to his conference table, and began unpacking the pastries and coffee.

"Chocolate doughnut or cheese Danish?" he asked politely, trying to regain control of the situation.

"Cheese Danish," Barnes said, noticing how quickly Peachwater had shifted his demeanor.

Peachwater placed the pastries and two large Styrofoam cups of coffee on the table and motioned for Barnes to join him. "I think we'll be comfortable here."

Barnes replaced the book on the shelf and sat down at the table. Peachwater politely waited for her to have the first bite and then sipped his coffee, thoughtfully.

"What makes an attractive woman like you become a police detective?" Peachwater asked with obvious interest.

"I've been asking myself that question lately," Barnes said reflexively. "But I'm not here to talk about me. I'm here to talk to you about Hillary Miles."

Peachwater cocked his head back. "Fire away."

Barnes had little use for and even less patience with bullshitters. And *my, oh, my, what a bullshitter* Peachwater was. He simply reeked of pomposity and a fake sincerity that was dangerously manipulative.

119

Barnes took a deep breath and mustered her focus. "How long did you know Hillary?"

Peachwater gazed thoughtfully at the ceiling. "A little over a year. I was appointed her advisor last fall when she was an incoming freshman."

"What was her major?"

"She was in the hard sciences. Chemistry or physics. One of those two."

"Was she a successful student?"

"I think so. She had no academic problems that I know of."

"Did she have any personal problems?"

"What exactly do you mean?" Peachwater cocked his head, furrowed his brow, and, like an evil magician, fabricated a look of compassionate concern.

The cat-and-mouse game was afoot. Barnes was determined to stay one step ahead. "I mean, did she confide in you—as her advisor?"

"Hillary never spoke to me about her personal life. We pretty much stuck to academics."

Barnes was dying to tell him that she knew otherwise but restrained herself. "Tell me, do you have any idea why someone would want to kill her?" Barnes emphasized the word *kill* ever so slightly.

Peachwater ceremoniously furrowed his brow again. "Kill her? What do you mean, kill her?"

"I'm sorry, Professor Peachwater. Didn't you know?"

Peachwater spoke very slowly and deliberately. "All I was told was that she died. It never occurred to me that she was murdered."

Detective Linda Barnes smiled sardonically. "Well, she was. And I want to find out who did it."

With a folded white napkin, Peachwater carefully removed a spot of coffee from his conference table. He pursed his lips with circumspection. "Ms. Barnes, I truly wish I could be of some help. But I really didn't know her that well."

Barnes sipped her coffee and placed the cup on the table. "I want to ask you a question about student-professor relationships here at Hopkins. Would you say many of them have a sexual component?"

"A sexual component?" Peachwater asked with exaggerated innocence.

"Yeah. Do the professors hit on the students much?" Barnes felt the question pierce Peachwater's armor.

"I wouldn't think so," Peachwater said indignantly. "Here at Hopkins we have the highest ethical standards. We take the business of education very seriously."

"But it does happen...doesn't it?"

"I really wouldn't know." Peachwater's demeanor was evident; he was shutting down right now!

Barnes leaned back in her chair. She felt her unbuttoned navy blazer taper open to reveal the curve of her bountiful breasts beneath her red striped blouse. She saw Peachwater's eyes divert, for a fraction of a second, to the attraction. "Let's just say I have reason to believe Hillary was having an affair with a faculty member."

Peachwater sat absolutely still. Like an ice sculpture. "How did you find that out?" he said with perceptible tightness in his voice.

Barnes had him worried. She knew it. He knew she knew it. She paused for effect. "I'm sorry, Professor. Confidential police information. I'm sure you understand."

Peachwater slowly pushed his chair back from the table, stretched out his legs, crossed his arms over his chest, and took an exasperated breath. "What does a faculty member having an affair with a student have to do with *murder*?"

"Nothing, maybe...but it might...considering that Hillary was pregnant."

Peachwater responded almost too quickly. "Detective Barnes, I have to admit this is all very disturbing. But I must tell you—the thought of a Hopkins faculty member murdering a student is just preposterous. I can only conclude that you have some *bad* information."

The interlocutors stared at one another, frozen in a battle of wits, each knowing the other suspected the worst. Barnes got up from her chair and extended her hand. "Professor, thanks for taking the time to talk with me."

"Well, I'm sorry I couldn't have been more helpful," Peachwater said, shaking her hand, squeezing it a bit too tightly.

Barnes walked briskly toward the door but then stopped and turned around. "There is one more thing. Do you know a Ms. Browning in the chaplain's office?"

Peachwater stroked his chin thoughtfully. "Browning...hmmm...you know the name does sound familiar." Peachwater cocked his head as if he were listening for an answer from somewhere in the atmosphere. "Ah...I know...a security guard mentioned that name to me in connection with a burglary in the chaplain's office...Browning...that was the name."

"So did you know her?"

"No."

Barnes nodded, with a look that said her time with him was over, and walked out the door. She moved quickly down the hall, around the corner, and down a flight of stairs. She wanted to leave her encounter with Peachwater open ended. She wanted to give him something to think about—like a tune that spontaneously repeats itself unmercifully in the mind.

Out in the Hopkins quadrangle, walking free in the fresh air, Barnes felt the heaviness in her chest lift. She had a frighteningly clear intuition that Peachwater was the man she was after—and yet, she had not one shred of evidence to incriminate him. Nothing. All she could do was wait and hope that something she may have overlooked would make itself apparent or that Peachwater would panic and do something self-defeating.

From the office window above, Peachwater watched Barnes cross the quadrangle and disappear from view. He felt a hard pulse in his temples and a raging storm whirling in his mind. Dark, macabre visions of Hillary and Lisa flashed across the worn and contaminated screen of his consciousness, and from some black, unnamable space in his heavy soul, a hideous, guttural laugh rose spontaneously.

42

Dean Viola Smith. Blue-haired veteran Dean of Students at the Johns Hopkins University. She sits quietly at her desk, sipping tea and reviewing budget projections for the coming year. She is a simple woman. Divorced at a young age. Childless. Bookish but not scholarly. For twenty-seven years, she has done her job at Hopkins and returned home to her cats and plants and British murder mysteries. She is not one to become embroiled in controversy.

The dean's secretary poked her head around the door. "Viola, Detective Barnes is here to see you."

"Okay. Send her in," Dean Smith said, getting up from her desk and approaching the door.

Barnes entered the comely office where she had interviewed Megan Drew and Jeff Danforth earlier in the week. The dean greeted her at the door with a hearty, and surprisingly masculine, handshake. "Would you care for tea or coffee?" Dean Smith asked, her right eye twitching nervously behind her wire-rimmed spectacles.

"Nothing, thank you," Barnes said. Barnes noticed a faint, unpleasant mustiness about the dean.

"Let's sit here," Dean Smith said, pointing to one of two black leather sofas forming a comfortable corner at the far end of the office.

Barnes fought back a mischievous smile as she sized up Dean Viola Smith. *Blue hair? Really! Musty smell. Right eye twitching away. Lips pursed together like a prune. Much too much rouge on her bony cheeks. The stylish academic,* she thought.

"I can't tell you how distressed I am over the death of Hillary Miles,"

Smith said. "To tell the truth, I never met her. But somehow, as Dean of Students, I feel curiously responsible. Do you understand what I mean?"

Barnes looked at the sheltered woman sitting across from her. "Yes, I do understand."

Dean Smith seemed a bit distracted. She removed her spectacles and dabbed at her twitching right eye with two fat fingers. "Well, that's the way it is."

Barnes reached into her blazer pocket for notepad and pen. "Dean Smith, I don't want to take too much of your time. I just have a few questions to ask you." The dean began wringing her hands unconsciously. "You mentioned that you never met Hillary Miles, so I'm concluding that you were never aware of any problems concerning her matriculation at Hopkins."

"Yes, that's correct."

"And no one else ever spoke to you about her?"

"No."

"Are you aware that Elliot Peachwater was Hillary's advisor?"

"Yes," Dean Smith said. The right side of her mouth was now quivering in syncopation with her twitching right eye. "Yesterday afternoon I familiarized myself with Hillary's school records. I did see that Professor Peachwater was her advisor. Why do you ask?"

"Well, let's say I'm just trying to cover all the bases."

Smith nodded and began fidgeting with her watchband.

"Now I have a few questions about Professor Peachwater. Tell me, have any complaints been brought against him...by either students or other professors?"

Smith stiffened. Barnes could smell the musty odor intensify as the dean started to perspire. "I'm a bit confused, Detective. Why are you asking questions about Professor Peachwater?"

Barnes snapped a look at the dean that said she meant business. "Let's just say I'm investigating those people who knew Hillary...those people who may have had some kind of relationship with her."

Smith pressed back against the sofa, her left eye open wide like a saucer, her right eye twitching away rhythmically.

"Tell me about Peachwater," Barnes said authoritatively.

Smith took a deep breath and rested her chin in the palm of her left hand. She looked like a fish pressing its face against the side of an aquarium. "Yes, there have been complaints from time to time."

"Please be specific."

"Well, there have never been any formal charges made. But I have been approached by a few students, all young women, concerning what they felt to be sexual misconduct."

"How many students have come to you?"

"I'm not sure...maybe four or five."

"Have you confronted Peachwater about this? Has he ever been reprimanded?"

Smith's left eye filled with tears. The right one twitched over a dry cornea. "No. I have never said anything to him."

Barnes shook her head. "Why the *hell* not?"

Smith slowly stood up. "Let me show you something."

The dean labored across the room and pulled a thin volume from a tall antique bookcase. She leafed through the pages. When she found what she wanted, she brought the book to Barnes.

"Detective, this is our annual Board of Regents publication. It shows the major benefactors that contribute to the University. Look for yourself." Smith handed the open book to Barnes and pointed to a particular line.

As Barnes silently read, Smith spoke: "As you can see, the Peachwater family has, for many years, supplied this University with generous funding. We're talking millions of dollars. It all comes from his mother. That's where the money is. I'm not proud to say this, but Professor Peachwater is untouchable. He's well protected from on high. Unless someone files a formal, corroborated complaint with an aggressive attorney at his or her side, nothing is going to happen."

Barnes nodded knowingly. "So your hands are tied by the University's purse strings?"

"Precisely."

"Ain't life beautiful?" Barnes quipped.

A worried pall cast itself like a dark shadow across the countenance, tics and all, of Dean Smith. "Detective, I love my job here at Hopkins. It's really my whole life. You're not going to..."

"Don't worry. I'm not going to go over your head on this. I see what it's all about."

"Thank you, Detective. Thank you very much." Dean Smith removed her glasses and covered her right eye with the palm of her right hand. "This is not good," Dean Smith muttered to herself. "This is not good."

Barnes got up and walked toward the door. As she passed the dean's desk, she saw several framed pictures of cats in different postures of repose. *Christ,* she thought, *Dean Smith's first line of communion is with her cats...How is she supposed to deal with Peachwater?* Barnes stopped at the office door and looked back at Dean Smith. The dean was rocking back and forth on the leather sofa. Making some low-grade humming sound. *I'll be damned,* she thought. *The old dean is purring.*

Detective Linda Barnes. Walking through the dean's outer office. Stopping at the secretary's desk. Leaning across the desk and winking at the officious woman sitting behind a mound of printouts. "I think your boss could use a saucer of milk."

43

Elliot Peachwater straightened his Italian Como silk tie before the gilt-edged mirror in his expansive, cedar dressing room. He studied himself carefully, and, upon deciding that he looked sharper than a tack in his midnight blue double-breasted Armani suit, walked confidently out of the dressing room, through the well-appointed bedroom, out into the hall, and down the stairway.

Long before he entered the kitchen, he could smell the delicate scents and aromas of fresh croissants and jam and coffee. Chelsea Thornton-Peachwater was perched perfectly in her chair at one end of the kitchen table, leafing through a Saks catalog. She was a natural blonde, very well coiffed, slim, still shapely. All in all, a well-preserved specimen of a Vassar-educated wife who never set foot in the world of gainful employment.

"Good morning, dear," Peachwater said to his wife, kissing her lightly on the cheek.

"Good morning," Chelsea said, not looking up from the catalog. "Jasmine prepared a lovely breakfast, don't you think?"

"Ah, yes. Lovely." Peachwater sat down at the opposite end of the table.

When Chelsea looked up, she was caught by surprise. "Elliot, don't you look divine!"

"Do you like the suit? It's new."

"It's absolutely scrumptious. You must have something important going on."

Peachwater feigned sadness. "Actually, I'm off to attend a funeral."

"My gracious! Who died?"

"One of my students. A young woman."

"Did I know her?"

"No, I don't believe you ever met her. In fact, outside of being her advisor, I hardly knew her. I just thought paying my respects would be the proper thing to do."

Chelsea gazed at the man she had been swooning over for the last twenty-five years. "I just think you're wonderful. I'm sure your presence will be uplifting to everyone."

Peachwater smiled, feigning a look of humility as he reached for a croissant. *It's truly amazing*, he thought, *that anyone could be as gullible and blind as this rich Vassar queen sitting before me.* Catching her eye, he wrinkled his nose playfully. *What a stupid cow*, he thought.

44

About thirty folding chairs were stationed before the lectern in the Garrett Room at the Johns Hopkins University. The urn holding the ashes of Lisa Browning sat on a small table situated directly in front of the lectern. At 10:50 a.m., people began to enter the room. Milling about and talking softly, friends and relatives of the deceased introduced themselves to one another, offered kind words of condolence, and eventually took seats.

At 10:58, Malcolm Storey, the elderly, white-haired chaplain of the University, entered the room from a side door, flanked by Father Byron and Detective Barnes. Storey and Barnes went to stand at the back of the room as Byron walked, respectfully, to the lectern. Byron carefully adjusted his vestments, checked his watch, and began. "Good morning to all of you. I'm Father Byron..."

Byron's words faded into the background as Barnes thought of Hillary Miles and *her* funeral service going on simultaneously across town. She wondered if Peachwater would show his face. She thought he would. That's why she had planted another detective at the Miles service. Just to watch. Just to observe Peachwater's actions and reactions.

Byron's soothing, melodious voice filtered back into Barnes' consciousness: "...what is important for us to come to terms with today is acceptance. Acceptance of what has taken place in the life of Lisa Browning, and acceptance of what has taken place in our own lives as a consequence of her death."

Barnes turned to the chaplain. "Reverend Storey, I've been meaning to ask you...do you ever get involved with the counseling done in your office?"

Storey shrugged his shoulders. There was something eternally sad about him. "No. I'm afraid I'm too old for that. I don't really connect anymore with the young people. I left the counseling to Lisa."

"Did Lisa ever speak to you about anyone she was counseling...you know, use you as a sounding board?"

"No. Lisa took the confidentiality thing very seriously...which was fine with me."

Byron's voice again claimed Barnes' attention. "If you are having trouble comprehending all of this, please know that you are not alone. We will never completely understand why Lisa felt the way she did. But we must accept that, for Lisa, her judgments about life were viable. It's my belief that she was extraordinarily brave and confident. Brave and confident enough to act in light of what she believed to be true and at the risk of being misunderstood and pitied."

Reverend Storey squeezed Barnes' arm. "This is the strangest memorial service I've ever heard."

Barnes smiled. "Why do you say that?"

"Oh, I don't know. It's just so unorthodox. No reading from the Bible. No mention of salvation. No explanation about what it all means. Hell, I guess he's just being honest."

Barnes nodded. "Yeah, I think that's what it is. He's just being honest."

Barnes surveyed the scene before her. Byron was talking to several people at the front of the room, handing out the suicide notes that had previously been confiscated by the police. Some people were slowly moving toward the door, others were frozen in their tracks—staring at the floor. Some were trying to make conversation about the unspeakable.

Reverend Storey again squeezed Barnes' arm. "Could I give you some friendly advice?"

Barnes looked at him quizzically. "I'm listening."

"Go home and get some sleep. You really seem exhausted."

Barnes smiled at the old man. "I would if I could. But I can't."

"Why not?"

"Nice people keep getting killed."

The old man nodded his head, shook her hand, and walked away.

45

After the funeral service, Barnes drove downtown to the precinct office and called Detective Mark Gregus at his home. "Mark? This is Linda Barnes."

"Hi, Linnba," Gregus mumbled into the phone. "Coul you holl on a sec?" Barnes held the phone and listened to thrashing noises. "Jesus, you caught me with a piece of saltwater taffy in my mouth. I had to spit it out."

"That stuff's no good for you. You should be glad I called."

"Yeah, yeah, I know. Look, your man showed up at the funeral."

"I'll be damned. I thought he would. Did he do anything interesting?"

"Not really...the usual stuff."

"Did he talk to Hillary's parents?"

"Yeah, he did. He was very courteous. Whatever he said seemed to comfort them."

"He's a real charmer, that one." The two held on in silence.

"Thanks for doing this on your day off. I owe you one," Barnes said and hung up the phone.

Barnes swallowed uncomfortably. Her throat constricted at the thought of Peachwater talking to Hillary's mother. When she had talked to Mrs. Miles earlier in the week, the bereaved told her she hoped that someone from Hopkins would tell her that her daughter was "wonderful." She needed to hear this because she didn't know who her daughter was any more. They had fallen out years ago. If Barnes was right, the one who comforted the mother had killed the daughter.

46

Detective Sergeant Rick Rogers looked up from his desk, squinted at the plastic clock hanging cock-eyed on the wall across from him, and barked, "Take a seat, Barnes. I'll be with you in a second."

Barnes sat in one of the two uncomfortable wooden chairs facing Rogers' desk. She stared at her squad supervisor as he sat hunched over a stack of police reports. Save a few strands of golden hair, he was bald. His skin was pale from lack of exposure to sunlight, and she could see his hands trembling ever so slightly as he fingered the documents.

"You need more light in here, Rick. It's like a dungeon."

Rogers said nothing. Just kept reading what was in front of him. After a few moments, he pushed the papers away and leaned back in his chair. He stared at Barnes with eyes that told a thousand stories of weariness.

"You know, I got three years until retirement. It doesn't sound like a very long time, does it? But I'll tell you something, Barnes, from where I sit, it looks like I'll never get there. Those fucking animals in the streets are getting worse and worse. Every fucking day there's another homicide report on my desk. I don't have enough goddamn cops to go around." Rogers suddenly stopped talking, put his elbows on his desk, clasped his hands together in front of his face, and peered out at Barnes over the top of his knuckles. "Okay, Barnes. What have you got for me? Something about a dead student and a suspicious suicide? Christ, you get the winners, don't you?"

Barnes looked at her long-time friend and shook her head. "Rick, when you retire, we're going down to the Marble Bar. I'll set 'em up while you knock 'em down."

"Sure, Barnes. When I retire."

Barnes pulled a notepad out of her inside blazer pocket and flipped through the pages. "Okay. Here's what I've got. On Monday, November 15th, around two a.m., a nineteen-year-old Hopkins undergrad by the name of Hillary Miles is suffocated in the bedroom of her off-campus apartment. No forced entry, no burglary, no sex with the victim, no witnesses. And today, I get the good news from the lab techs that there were no readable prints in the apartment other than the victim's."

Rogers pulled a half-smashed pack of Camels from the breast pocket of his yellowed white shirt. "You still smoke?"

Barnes shook her head no. "Plitt's autopsy gives me the only lead I can work with. The girl was five weeks pregnant. So I go on a wild goose chase in the city trying to track down the clinic that was taking care of the victim's gynecological needs. I thought she might have been seeking advice on the pregnancy, and maybe she mentioned the guy who knocked her up. No luck, though. These clinics aren't much on recordkeeping, and the docs and nurses are short on memory."

Lighting up one of the Camels, Rogers gestured with his hand for her to continue.

"When I did some interviews at Hopkins, I found out that a few days before her death, a file on Hillary was stolen from the chaplain's office. Hillary was undergoing counseling with Lisa Browning, the director of Student Life, who happens to work out of the chaplain's office. I'll get back to that in a minute. I also found out that Hillary might have been having an affair with an older, married man...a theology professor. I don't have to tell you how that piqued my interest...but I'll get back to him too."

Rogers, unconsciously gnawing on one of the knuckles of his left hand, indicated with his eyes that he was following her.

"Okay. Now on Wednesday morning, November 17th, at about one a.m., a middle-aged woman appears to commit suicide with a Smith and Wesson handgun. The woman's name is Lisa Browning...sound familiar?"

Rogers picked a piece of tobacco off of his tongue. "Small world, isn't it?"

"Now listen to this. When I get to the crime scene, there's a Catholic priest there. He found the body. He tells me he had just met Lisa a few days before. He also tells me that she had *planned* to commit suicide, but in his opinion she had not!"

"Hold on there, Barnes. What do you mean she planned to commit suicide?"

"It may sound strange, but the priest said she discussed it with him. He just didn't interfere."

Rogers rubbed out his cigarette in a narrow, yellow ashtray sitting on the end of his desk. Under the ashes, Barnes could make out the words *Gunther Beer* written in blue script. "Jesus Christ! What's this world coming to? Look, Barnes, how do we know this wacko priest didn't do it?"

Barnes looked at Rogers with fierce defensiveness. "Believe me, he didn't."

Rogers stared at her, unconvinced.

"Look, can we get on with this?"

"Go on."

"I've been suspicious about this so-called suicide from the start. The priest says Lisa would never have resorted to a violent suicide, and I have to agree. After reading the suicide notes she prepared for family and friends, there's no way she's going to blow her brains out. This woman was going to do it with pills or by injection. But, of course, when we do a sweep of the apartment, we don't find any evidence of pills or a serum."

Rogers rolled his eyes. "It's a red ball, Barnes."

Barnes nodded her head. "The other thing that bothered me was the way the .22 was conveniently dangling from the woman's hand. It's too much like Hollywood. And, of course, I turn out to be right when Plitt tells me that the head wound is inconsistent with a suicide."

"Okay, Barnes, I get the point. Tell me, where are you going with all this?"

"Well, our check for prints and registration on the .22 came up negative. But I'll tell you, Rick, I got a strong hunch that our theology professor is in real deep."

"Well, be careful. We could look like real assholes if we don't watch ourselves. We don't want any defamation-of-character crap around here. You understand?"

"Yeah, I understand."

Rogers cautiously leaned sideways in his chair. *Damn hemorrhoids.* "So what's this hunch about?"

"Elliot Peachwater is a professor of theology at Hopkins. A real highbrow. The word is that Hillary was sweet on him. He was her advisor. I also hear that Peachwater has a habit of hitting on the coeds."

139

"Hold on, Barnes. Who are your sources on this?"

"I think they're reliable. Hillary's best friend told me about Hillary's attraction to Peachwater, and the priest told me about Peachwater hitting on the coeds."

"God damn it, Barnes! You're losing me. How does the priest know about Peachwater?"

"He used to teach with him at Georgetown."

Rogers shook his head. "All right. Go on."

"Here's the way I think everything plays out: Peachwater and Hillary are having a good old time. But then the rabbit dies, and Peachwater gets shaky. I imagine the two of them talk things out. Peachwater wants a surreptitious abortion, and Hillary wants the baby. Now you've got to understand, Peachwater is used to getting his own way. He has a pristine image to protect. Respected professor, devoted husband and father—at least that's the way he sees it. So having the baby is out of the question. Now somewhere along the line, Hillary tells him she has confided in someone else about all of this. Peachwater finds out it's Browning, and the killings begin."

"Okay, I get the picture. Have you've talked to Peachwater?"

"You bet I have."

"And?"

"Annnd, I think he did it. He's slimy and he's shrewd. And you know what else? I spoke with the Dean of Students at Hopkins and found out that there have been several informal complaints of sexual misconduct against him. The problem is that his family has thrown millions of dollars at the University. To make a long story short, he's untouchable."

Rogers' chair squeaked violently as he got up. A grimace spread across his face as he massaged his lower back. "Ah, Barnes, I guess you just have to wait it out and hope he makes a mistake. But I've got to tell you—I can't keep you on this case forever. You're going to have to squeeze this bastard. And if he doesn't break, it's just another red ball that goes back into the files." Rogers sucked at one of his upper molars as his eyes glassed over. "Those fucking animals out there are on the loose. You know, it scares me. I don't feel safe walking to my car at night."

Barnes stood and looked at the beaten-down man before her. *Dark nights of the soul to us all*, she thought. She waved good-bye as she walked out the door.

Rogers returned to his seat and reached into his top desk drawer for aspirin. The faint smell of perfume lingered. "Goddamn good woman," he said out loud.

47

Driving north on Charles Street, Linda Barnes watched the orange autumn sun descend into the outer reaches of the afternoon rush hour. Normally, the heavy traffic would have provoked Barnes, but today her mind was on what was to come at the end of the drive. She was going to see Peachwater. At his home. Uninvited. She hoped to catch him by surprise. She also hoped Mrs. Peachwater would be there.

Linda Barnes slowed down at the intersection of Art Museum Drive and Charles Street. She did this to have a better look at the statue adjacent to the main entrance to the Johns Hopkins University. For as long as she could remember, the bronze nude female was blackened with soot—all but her bountiful breasts, which were polished to a bright, gleaming gold. As she passed the sculpture, Barnes laughed at the spectacle and thought of the hundreds of young JHU fraternity boys who had had their way with that still and dignified lady.

Turning right on 39th Street and left on Greenway, Barnes drove her less-than-elegant Jeep into the land of the wealthy. The sheer gigantism of the homes and gardens made her wonder what it must be like to be raised and groomed in families of old money, generation after generation of money and education and culture. Back in the palatial streets off Greenway Drive, there were no nouveaux riches. Only old money was allowed. Only old money could survive.

Pulling up to the curb in front of Peachwater's house, Barnes could feel her heart kick into overdrive. Ever since she got the idea of the surprise visit to Peachwater's home, she acted as if she knew what she was doing. Now she knew she was wrong. This was nothing more than a last-ditch effort to try to force Peachwater into some slip of the tongue, some mental error that would give her something to work on. Walking toward the entrance of the Peachwater mansion, she recognized she had no idea what she would do or say when that heavy, ornate door opened wide.

Barnes rang the bell. After about fifteen seconds, Jasmine, the live-in housekeeper and cook, answered the door. Jasmine wore a finely tailored, dark blue suit and crisp, white, high-collared blouse. When she spoke, it was with a strikingly beautiful African-British accent that was simultaneously seductive and pleasing to the ear.

"Hello, madam. How may I help you?"

"Hello," Barnes said, somewhat surprised by the polished presentation of the woman standing before her. "My name is Linda Barnes. I'm a detective with the Baltimore City Police Department." Barnes efficiently presented identification from her inside blazer pocket. "I'm here to see Professor Peachwater. Is he home?"

Jasmine nodded and beckoned Barnes into the opulent entrance hall. "Please wait here while I find the professor."

Barnes grew numb as she watched Jasmine walk past a magnificent marble staircase and disappear through an ornate archway. The foyer was of such magnitude, Barnes succumbed to a natural inclination to look up—and when she did, she saw thirty-foot frescoed ceilings join the Romanesque hand-painted walls. Antique sideboards displaying an eclectic combination of Greek, Roman, and Oriental vases lined the walls surrounding her.

What the fuck am I doing here? she thought, her eyes dwelling on her scuffed, black loafers as they contrasted dramatically with the pristine, polished marble floor. Shaking her head and biting her lip, Linda could hear the precise clicking of Jasmine's heels. When she looked up, the housekeeper stopped and silently motioned for her to follow.

The two women, one after the other, navigated the first floor of that monstrous house through a maze of hallways, all of which led into spacious, finely decorated rooms, quaint nooks, and tasteful outside gardens. Finally, at the far end of the house, Jasmine waved Barnes through a door and into the study of Professor Peachwater.

There he was, sitting comfortably by the fireplace in a rich cordovan leather chair. As she approached, Peachwater rose and extended his hand. As he shook her hand, he held it just a little too long and looked into her eyes with an air of controlled anger and defiance. "Detective Barnes. In the future, if you wish to see me, I want you to make an appointment through my secretary at the University. Is that clear?"

This was just the kind of response Barnes was hoping for. She had caught him off guard. "Yes, it is," Barnes said. "I certainly wouldn't want to do anything to upset you."

"I'm *not* upset," Peachwater answered with perceptible tightness in his voice.

"Well, good," Barnes said, staring him down. "I just want to ask you a few questions. If you don't mind?"

"I don't mind, Detective. In fact, I find our conversations rather amusing."

"Amusing? You find murder amusing? I would think a specialist in ethics would find murder anything but amusing."

Peachwater's face contorted into a macabre grimace. Barnes could see he was trying to show her a relaxed smile, as if she had completely misunderstood him, but the anger beneath the facial mask betrayed him. When he spoke, his voice was loud and strained. "What I find amusing, Detective, is your wasted tenacity. What is it that you think I know? What is it that you think I've done?"

Barnes stared at him, eyes locked on his. "That's what I want you to tell me, Professor. What *have* you done?"

"What I've *done*, Detective, is cooperate with *you*! But, I must admit you're trying my patience now. If you have something specific to ask me, do it!"

As Peachwater spoke, Barnes saw what he didn't. Chelsea Thornton-Peachwater had entered the room. Barnes let Peachwater hang silent for a moment. "I do have something specific to ask you. But first, I'd like to be introduced to your wife."

Peachwater wrenched his neck around quickly. Chelsea stood at attention, perfectly displayed in white, double-breasted jacket, black skirt, black scarf, black nylons, and black, high-heeled shoes. The diamonds on her hands and earlobes flashed at her slightest movement.

"Elliot, Jasmine said you were talking with a police detective. What in the world is going on?"

In all her years on this earth, Barnes had never seen anything like Chelsea Thornton-Peachwater. It was as if she were not quite human. She seemed like some kind of high-tech, mechanical doll—perfect skin, perfect hair, perfect nails.

Peachwater, trying to pull himself together, turned to his wife. "Honey, this is Detective Barnes. I'm answering some questions regarding the student who died. Do you remember my telling you about her?"

Chelsea answered dutifully. "Oh, of course, dear. I remember."

Peachwater smiled at Barnes and mockingly blinked his eyes. Barnes, who felt like punching his face in, took a few steps back. She wanted to keep both Peachwaters in view.

"Professor, where were you between two and three a.m. on Monday, November 15th?" The room was silent. Like death. "And where were you between one and two a.m. on Wednesday, November 17th?"

Peachwater looked at Barnes with cold, black eyes, the eyes of a shark moving in on some bloody mass. "What do you *mean,* where was I?" Barnes stared at him silently, coldly. "I was here. In my study. Working."

Barnes turned quickly to Chelsea. "Can you corroborate that, Mrs. Peachwater?"

"Yes," Chelsea responded instantly.

"You can?" Barnes said, somewhat surprised. "Do you always stay up until three in the morning while your husband is working?"

"No, but I always wake up during the early morning hours. And when I do, I get up and bring Elliot to bed. It's bad for his back to fall asleep at his desk."

Barnes gave a hard glance at Peachwater, who was trying not to grin from ear to ear. "And you're sure that on these two mornings your husband was in his study?"

"Yes."

"How can you be so sure?"

"*Because I am.*"

The conversation was over. Barnes knew it. Peachwater knew it. Barnes took a deep breath and smiled bravely. "Well, I want to thank both of you for talking with me. I can find my way out."

As she walked toward the door of the study, her legs felt as if they weighed a thousand pounds. She could feel four eyes stabbing deep into her back, and wanted more than anything to simply disappear into thin air. But even before she reached the door, she knew there was one final humiliation to endure. Turning in the doorway, she once again faced the Peachwaters. "On second thought, I don't think I *can* find my way out."

48

Chelsea Thornton-Peachwater poured the last bit of Chateauneuf-du-Pape into her husband's wineglass. She really loved her man. After all, he fulfilled all of her expectations. She would say that she truly could not live without him.

"Elliot, why do you think that police woman was so rude to you? Asking those implicating questions!"

Peachwater looked at his wife through a haze of pleasant drunkenness. "I think it's all very obvious to see, Chelsea. Detective Barnes gets turned on when she makes powerful men squirm. The problem is I don't squirm. I think this is a case of a not-very-bright detective getting into something way over her head. Somehow, I don't think she'll be bothering us anymore."

"I still don't understand. Why was she asking you where you were in the middle of the night?"

Peachwater raised an index finger in front of Chelsea's eyes. "Now listen carefully, Chelsea," Peachwater said, as if talking to a grade-school student. "I will explain it only one more time. Detective Barnes is just a cop, which means she's not too bright to begin with. She's also a ball-buster, which means she likes to bring down men who are powerful and intelligent and successful. You see, Chelsea, I'm a threat to her. I'm everything she's not."

Peachwater paused a moment and sipped his wine. "Detective Barnes is simply pissing in the wind. And I must admit, Chelsea, when you told her I was at home on those two nights, I had to feel sorry for her. I mean, it's really sad to see someone trying to be clever and having their own piss blow back in their face." Peachwater was giggling now. "And my God, Chelsea, when you gave her that ironclad alibi, it must have seemed like a gale wind coming at her."

Peachwater looked at his devoted and very rich wife. *Christ,* he thought, *she has no idea what I'm talking about.* "Chelsea, let's just say that Detective Barnes has no one else to pick on. So she tried screwing with me. And now, she knows not to do it anymore. Okay?"

Chelsea moved closer to her husband on the love seat. "Elliot, I want you to know I did come down and wake you those two mornings. Just like I do every morning."

"Of course you did, dear. And I appreciate that. You know how stiff my back gets if I fall asleep at my desk."

"Yes, that's right," Chelsea said mindlessly. "Well, I think I'll turn in. I've got to go to Cross Keys tomorrow morning. Octavia is holding an absolutely precious dress for me."

"Ah, very good. Well, I'll be up in a moment, dear. Just want to read a bit before I turn in."

Chelsea Thornton-Peachwater kissed her husband lightly on the cheek and disappeared out of the soft light of the study. Peachwater sat very still, staring into space. His mind assumed a happy blank for a few seconds, and then reality moved back into view. Next to the empty bottle of Chateauneuf-du-Pape was a familiar and telltale sign of Chelsea Thornton-Peachwater—a half-empty bottle of Bombay Sapphire Gin. Peachwater's wife was a gin alcoholic—a pleasant one, no doubt, but an alcoholic nonetheless. This fact was never mentioned in the Peachwater household and certainly nowhere else. *And as it turned out,* Peachwater mused, *it's all for the best.* For many years now, Chelsea would drink herself into sweet oblivion every night, go to bed with a happy conscience, and sleep heavily straight through until morning. And for many years now, Elliot Peachwater would, for his own *very* necessary benefit, sustain the masquerade of thanking his wife in the morning for thoughtfully coming to wake him from his intellectually induced, late-night slumbers. It all worked out so well. Peachwater could duck out for his nocturnal liaisons and, at the same time, convince his wife of her loving kindness. *Yes, yes,* thought Peachwater, *life is good.*

49

Dean Viola Smith finished her second cup of Twinings English Breakfast tea. Under normal circumstances, she would never drink tea at 11:30 on a school night. The caffeine would make her restless, and sleep would be hard to come by. This, however, was no normal evening.

Under normal circumstances, Dean Viola Smith would enjoy her tea with a scoop of sugar and a splash of cream. And only the Claremont Rose English bone china teacup and saucer would accompany her to the parlor. This evening, however, she had brought with her a silver tray holding teapot, teacup, saucer, an entire carton of cream, and four small china bowls. She was having, as it were, a final tea party—with her four cats.

Dean Viola Smith in her red flannel nightgown and black leather slippers, regally enthroned on her Firenze Studio Scandinavian sofa of sleek, white leather, held court with her four gray Maine Coon cats: Marie Antoinette (Viola's favorite heroine), Chardonnay (Viola's favorite wine), Simone (as in de Beauvoir, Viola's favorite scholar), and Boysenberry (Viola's favorite jam). All four cats, well fed and quite robust, sat at attention before her. Each cat had before it a cleanly licked bowl, and each cat continued to lick spasmodically at its lips in order to savor and prolong the generous offering of sweet cream.

"Do you hear what we're listening to, my babies?" Viola asked her four furry loved ones. "It's *Death and Transfiguration* by Schubert. Isn't it lovely?"

Marie Antoinette, Chardonnay, and Boysenberry looked off into empty space with great concentration. Simone, however, looked deeply into Viola's eyes (the right one twitching away like a flashing light) and seemed to nod in agreement.

Viola smiled with great satisfaction. All was as it should be. "I'm playing this marvelous piece of music because this is the evening of *my* death and transfiguration. Or, more correctly, *our* death and transfiguration." Viola Smith dabbed at her lower lip with the fingertips of both hands. "I would never leave you here without me, my babies."

Marie Antoinette, Chardonnay, and Boysenberry continued to stare intently at imaginary objects floating in space. Simone, on the other hand, was getting anxious. Her left eyebrow rose with anticipation.

"Very soon, we will all go to sleep. And we will have a wonderful dream together. And we will live in that dream forever, never to wake up again." Dean Viola Smith felt her eyes swimming gently in their loose, rubbery sockets. "To make a long story short, my dear babies, old Viola has been a bad dean. She has allowed a bad man to hurt her students. And she just can't do anything about it!"

Marie Antoinette, Chardonnay, and Boysenberry yawned in unison. Simone, quite to the contrary, began to back away with circumspection. She cocked her fat, furry face in disbelief, as if to say, *You've got to be fucking kidding!*

"So what I've done, my babies, is give all of us access to our long dream together. No one will be left behind. We have all had quite a potent dose of sleeping pills. Mine, crushed up finely in my tea, and yours, crushed up finely in your cream." Dean Viola Smith began to teeter on the edge of the sofa. Her right eye twitched no more. She smiled reflexively as an elastic string of clear drool dropped from the corner of her mouth. "I'm such a poet," she giggled. "The finely crushed pills have ushered us into the finest of places with finality."

Dean Viola Smith fell to the floor with a thud. Marie Antoinette,

Chardonnay, and Boysenberry curled up together and took a long, last, deep breath. Simone was in the kitchen puking up a hairball, along with other sundry contents of her stomach. After the retching was over, she bounded out to the parlor and stared intently at the lifeless bodies garnishing the floor. She meowed loudly and flipped over on her back. Staring meaningfully at the empty space above her, she happily shifted her attention to her two front paws, playfully reaching out into the void without fear or remorse.

50

The call on the police radio barked, "Monster down. Alley north of Preston and Howard. Requesting Detective Linda Barnes for investigative expertise."

Barnes shook her head and laughed. *Christ, what could **this** be about?* Quickly glancing in the rearview mirror and pumping the accelerator, she sped around a car and took off into the left lane. The digital clock on the dashboard of the Jeep read 1:00 a.m. A light frost had formed on the windows of the parked cars on either side of the street, and the moon was out, full and bright. Only winos, junkies, and drug dealers were about in the dark, cold grayness of the *City That Reads*.

Barnes was one of the few Baltimore City homicide detectives who traveled alone. She had partnered in the past with a couple of different guys. But it just never worked out. There was always some murky sexual tension—or maybe it was sexist tension—that made concentrated police work impossible. She often reflected on how odd it was that she rarely felt afraid moving about alone in this hellhole of a city where knives, guns, and metal pipes were sported as commonly as cheap costume jewelry on a teenage harlot. Seven years in homicide had a way of deadening the soul to fear—or maybe the fear was so all-consuming, so grotesquely routine, that it was simply no longer noticed.

Turning into the alley north of Preston and Howard Streets, Barnes met the bright lights of a squad car and an ambulance. Pulling up next to the ambulance, Barnes saw two homicide detectives from her unit sitting on the back bumper, drinking coffee. She rolled down her window. "What the hell's going on here? Why did you call *me* in on this?"

The two detectives looked at each other. *What, me worry?* The cop closer to Barnes smiled sardonically. "We just thought you'd like to see this one for yourself."

Barnes got out of her car and slammed the door. "You guys are really sick, you know that? I've got better things to do besides coming here to look at *your* John Doe lying in an alley."

"Ah, come on, Barnes. Just take a look. Maybe you can help us out with this one. The body is over there in the gutter."

Flashing lights—red, blue, white—reflected off the wet brick walls and cobblestone alley like an invitation to a carnival of the grotesque. The stink of rotting garbage pervaded the air. A rat streaked by in search of something to live for. Barnes approached the body. A sick feeling descended upon her. Homicide cops were known for their less-than-sophisticated sense of humor. She really had no idea what she would find.

But suddenly, it was all there in front of her. The nude body of a black male lay in the gutter, legs twisted grotesquely beneath him. Black plastic batwings were attached to his arms, and long, red plastic fingernails adorned his lifeless hands. A two-foot, wooden stake protruded from his chest. Blood ran wildly down the gutter, mingling with the rainwater and urine and wine that routinely ribbon through alleys of this sort. The victim's head lay two feet from the body, cut clean off by some ravenous blow. The mouth of the severed head was stuffed with garlic and gave off a rank odor that spoke of some yellow, foul insanity running loose like a plague in the city.

Standing over the mangled, lost soul, Barnes could feel herself wanting to heave with laughter. It was just so goddamned pitiful. Some crazed lunatic saving the city from vampires. One freak feeding on another. In the end, no great loss.

Barnes walked back and joined the two detectives. The three of them stared at each other with deadpan expressions, eyeing each other heavily to see which one would crack first. After about fifteen seconds, Barnes lost it and the others followed suit. The three cops wailed hysterically, violently, lungs heaving to catch a breath of air. Holding each other up to keep from falling down, the three macabre figures carried out what looked like some strange, aboriginal, incongruous dance of pain and suffering and camaraderie and survival. The full moon above illuminated it all.

Back in her car, driving north on Charles Street, Barnes knew she was in trouble. The trouble was deep within her. Over the years, working homicide had systematically gutted her of any sustained spiritual or moral fiber. The tension of her own inwardness had become so tight that it strangled her. Now there were just fragments of memories of what life used to be, of what she used to long for: love, happiness, a sense of belonging, a sense of completion. Now there was nothing but darkness inside. Emptiness. Demons of doubt. And, yes, something else. *Some evil edge.* Something she didn't want to encounter.

Swallowing hard, she asked herself, *What am I going to do?*

She waited and listened. No answer came forth.

51

Linda Barnes turned off the ignition to the Jeep. She stared through the passenger window at the bar across the street. The Midtown Yacht Club. A cop bar. A place where that which can never be spoken of is spoken of. She wondered what Rick Rogers wanted from her. When a cop told you to meet him at the Yacht Club, you showed up.

Barnes walked across Centre Street. No traffic. Soft light from the streetlamps showered down the red brick walls of old historic buildings harboring ancient secrets. A chill in the air. Faint sounds of a string quartet wafted through the night from a second-story window. The Peabody School of Music. Barnes stood like a statue in the middle of the street. Taking it all in. *How utterly bizarre*, she thought. *Last night at this time, a few blocks away, a vampire cadaver. Now the pleasantness of a peaceful village. Go figure...*

The Yacht Club was loud and crowded. Barnes spotted Rogers at the far end of the bar. He was hunched over his draft beer, peering into the glass vessel as if he had lost something dear to him.

"Hey, Rick. How's it going?"

Rogers slowly raised his head. He had been there awhile. "Hey, Barnes. Pull up a stool." He carefully surveyed her. "Looking good, as usual."

"Thanks. What's on tap?"

"Hell, you know me. I just drink Bud. I don't much care about the other stuff."

Barnes caught the attention of the bartender and yelled, "A pint of Bass with a Jack chaser." She squeezed Rogers' elbow. "So what's so important? You sounded a bit worried on the phone."

Rogers wiped his mouth with the back of his hand. "Remember when we rode together? You were just a rookie then."

Barnes laughed. "Don't remind me."

"I'll never forget the night we were called to Greenmount and 33rd." Rogers peered down the bar and caught the eye of the bartender. "Hey, Billy, come here a second."

The bartender approached, towel slung around his neck. His T-shirt read *Fuck Irsay!* "Whatcha need, Rick?"

Rick Rogers leaned forward as a wide, drunken smile spread across his face. "Billy, I want to tell you about one of the nights Barnes and I were riding together. We were dispatched to the corner of Greenmount and 33rd to referee a domestic disturbance. Well, we pull up to the corner, and there's this black guy, stark naked, standing in front of Uncle Lee's Restaurant. His wife has him pinned up against the glass window. She's got a fucking machete in her hand. I'm not kidding. A goddamn machete."

Rogers peered up and down the bar, as if what he was about to say were a state secret. "Well, we get out of the car, and we're moving in real slow. Trying to get an angle on her. Then, all of a sudden, the guy takes off! Running like a track star. Well, hell, she takes off after him. Here's this skinny little woman in a flannel nightgown running like hell after her man!" Rogers turned to Barnes. "Am I lying, Barnes? Am I?"

Barnes shook her head. "Nope. You're telling it just the way it happened."

Rogers smiled. He seemed pleased with himself. "So she's chasing him up the street. And Barnes and I are doing our best to keep up with them. The next thing I see is this *flash of silver*—just this *flash of silver light*.

"Well, Jesus Christ, she had brought that machete down on him in full stride. Tomahawked his left arm clean off at the shoulder. I'm half a block away, and I can see the blood spurting in the air like a geyser.

"Well, what happens next, I can hardly believe! The two of them stop cold in their tracks. They're just standing there looking at each other. Nobody's moving. Blood squirting up in the air. Then, all of a sudden, this fucker reaches down and picks up his arm. It was just lying there on the sidewalk. He picks it up and takes a swing at her head. Next thing I know, he's chasing her back down the street, and they're coming right at us. I wanted to shit in my pants. Here's this skinny black lady in her flannel nightgown running like hell straight at me. She's screaming her head off and still carrying that huge knife."

Barnes. Laughing so hard, she's gasping for air. "Oh, my God, Rick, please stop. I can't breathe."

Rogers, Barnes, and Billy. Hunched forward over the bar. Laughing, hysterically. Sucking wind to catch their breath.

"Billy, I swear it's all true," Barnes said. "It was just insane." Barnes looked at Rogers and nodded her head. "Okay, go on. Finish the story."

Rogers swallowed the last of his beer. A wide, mischievous smile spread across his face. "So here she comes, straight at me with that big machete. And the big, nakcd, black dude is chasing her like a freight train. I'm thinking I better go down like a tight end and block her. Well, the next thing I know, I see that arm whipping through the air like a windmill. I'm telling you, he clubbed her right in the head—

hard! Knocked her down on the ground.

"Now he's standing over her. He's got this black hole where his left shoulder used to be, and blood is gushing out everywhere. She's staring up at him, and he's standing over her, and nobody's moving. All of a sudden, I hear this little, squeaky voice coming from down on the ground. It says, *"I'm sorry, baby! I'm sorry, baby!"* The big guy is standing over her. He's holding this big, bloody stump in his right hand. He's breathing real hard. And then he says, *"No problem, baby. No problem."* Then the fucker falls forward on top of her. Dead as they get. And that was that. Case closed!"

Barnes threw back the Jack chaser. "When we did the autopsy on the husband, we knew why he was running around with one arm and not feeling the pain. Totally wired on morphine."

Rogers leaned forward. Eyes red. Smacking his lips. Smelling of stale beer. "Some slick lawyer got her off on an insanity plea. She's sitting over there in Crownsville as we speak."

Calls for Billy wafted through the air. The bartender saluted Rogers with good-natured mock respect. "Thanks for the story. I've got to get back."

Rogers looked at Barnes. His eyes were swollen with sadness. "Those were the days."

"Yep. We had some good times," Barnes said.

Rogers looked around the room. "Let's take a booth over there. I got something to tell you."

The two cops made their way through the crowd. Peanut shells covered the floor and crunched beneath their shoes. A haze of psychic tension filled the place. It was all too familiar.

Rogers pointed to a rear corner. "Take the booth back there. I'll get us a pitcher of beer."

Barnes slid lightly along the worn pew-like bench of the enclosure and fingered the dull and scratched surface of the wooden table before her. A history of libations, and stories told under the influence of such, permeated the booth. At the Yacht Club, the stories were more about sadness and failure than anything else.

"Here you go, Barnes." Rogers plunked two glasses and a pitcher of Bud on the table. He winced as he sat down. "Goddamn back. It hurts all the time."

Barnes filled both glasses with beer. "So what's up, Rick?"

Rogers surveyed the room as if he were expecting someone to be eavesdropping. He folded his massive arms on the table and stared down, seeing only oblivion. "I got myself a little problem. Actually, it's more than a little problem. Christ, Barnes, I don't know where to begin."

Barnes reached across the table and touched his arm. "Look at me, Rick. Look at me!" Rogers looked up. "You know you can tell me anything. It's all staying here at this table."

Rogers sighed, leaned forward with circumspection, and whispered, "Barnes, I've killed somebody. Killed him, chopped him up, and buried him."

Barnes leaned back as if being pushed by an invisible hand. "Oh, for God's sake, Rick! What the fuck are you saying?"

Rogers rubbed his eyes with the palms of his large, meaty hands. "Do you know how many animals out there on the street get away with their shit? Do you? Those animals are ruining other people's lives every day, and we don't even know about it. Yeah, we catch a few of them. Big deal! Most of them, we never even hear about."

Barnes held up her hand. "Rick, tell me what you did."

Rogers scratched at the late-night stubble of beard on his chin. "All right. I got a neighbor next door. A nice lady. Doesn't mean any harm to anybody. But she's got one bastard of a son. He milks her like an old cow. He's a crack addict. Always stealing money from her. Christ, he even stole the TV right out of her living room. All to pay for his habit. Well, this has been going on for years. I've talked to her. Told her I'd help her. But she keeps thinking her bastard of a son is going to kick the habit."

Rogers picked at a front tooth with his fingernail. "Well, a week ago, I come home and see an ambulance parked outside her house. I run over to see what happened, and they're hauling her out on a stretcher. She's nothing but a bloody pulp. I tell the medics I'm a cop, and they let me talk to her for just a second. You know what she says to me? She says, *'Don't hurt him. He's a good boy down under. He really didn't know what he was doing. He didn't mean to hurt me.'*"

Barnes shook her head and took a slug of beer. "We've heard that crap before."

"Well, Barnes, for me it was the last straw with this creep. I know where he hangs out. I know where he lives. I've got to tell you, I was calm. As calm and cool as could be. I waited until the street cleared. I had a ham and cheese sandwich. Drank a Bud. Watched a rerun of *Welcome Back, Kotter.* Then I went out to the shed. Got my hunting knife, a shovel, and a roll of plastic. Hopped in the car and off I went.

"I lured the fucker into the alley behind Archer's Bar in Dundalk. I took care of him quickly with the knife, threw him in the trunk of my Chevy, and drove out to my sister's farmhouse in Belair.

162

"Sis lives in Florida in the fall and winter, so there's nobody out there now. She's got this great little log chopper in the back. Rusted out a bit but works good enough. I ran that sorry bastard through the chopper. Hauled away the pieces in a plastic bag. Buried him in the woods. When I was finished, the sun was coming up. I went back to my sister's, gave the Chevy a good washing, and had breakfast at Roy Rogers."

Rogers picked at his left ear. "I like those little sausages at Roy's. Crispy but not too crispy."

Barnes took a deep breath. "Well, I'm glad you enjoyed your breakfast." Rogers drained his entire glass of beer with one swing of his forearm. "Rick, does anybody have any idea you might be involved?"

Rogers poured another glass of beer. "I don't think so. I think I'm home free." A look of despair cascaded across his face. "The problem is the guilt. I didn't know I could do such a thing. I'm really no better than the animals on the street."

Barnes leaned forward. "Rick, there's a *fine* line between us and them. I hate to admit it, but it's true. But remember, it's that fine line that counts."

Rogers' eyes filled with tears. "Do you think any less of me?"

"No, Rick. I don't think any less of you." Barnes compassionately placed her hand on his arm. "I think what happens is that we get worn down. We get hit with the shit over and over. And it never stops. And then, we say *enough!*" Barnes gently squeezed his arm. "Look at me, Rick. Look me in the eye." Rogers' eyes met hers. "When we say *enough*, we mean it. We no longer have a choice. We make what's wrong, right. Somebody's got to do it."

Rogers dropped his gaze back to the table. "Somehow, I've got to last until retirement. I need that pension."

"You'll make it, Rick. Just a few more years." Barnes released her grip on his arm. "Hell, Rick, we're all hitting the wall. You're not alone." Barnes leaned back and felt the wooden booth cut into her shoulder blades. "How long has it been since Marie died?"

Rogers took a deep breath. "Oh, about six years."

"You miss her?"

"She was a good woman. I think I miss her."

"Yeah, I think you do."

52

Detective Linda Barnes sat in her Jeep at the corner of Cathedral and Mulberry Streets and tried to compose herself. An unexpected and unwarranted fit of laughter had overtaken her. Part of her thought it was *oh, so funny*. Another part of her looked on in fear and desperation.

It was midnight. A cold mist hovered in the air, and a hard frost had begun to form on the streets and sidewalks. Several streetlamps were out, making the darkness of the night an uneasy specter. Barnes gazed through the window of her Jeep at the Basilica of the Assumption of the Blessed Virgin Mary. The dark portico of the old cathedral was curiously illuminated by sparks of light randomly moving about like fireflies.

Barnes stepped out of the Jeep, swallowed her laughter, and assumed the pose of concerned detective. As she climbed the stairway to the portico, she felt as if she were breaking up inside.

Detective Mark Gregus momentarily shined his flashlight at her. "Hey, Linda."

"Hey, Mark. So what's this about?"

Gregus sadly shook his head. "You Catholic?"

Detective Barnes shrugged her shoulders. "I'm not anything."

For a moment, Gregus stood in silence. "Hell, I'm not anything either. But I was raised Catholic." He stared down at his feet. "For some reason, this kind of shit really bothers me."

Barnes looked at the residue of mayhem festooning the portico. Six street cops were using flashlights to illuminate the carnage. In the weirdly clarified darkness, she could see the mutilated bodies of dead animals—they looked like baby lambs. They had been bludgeoned to death and strung with thin, silver wires around the ten fluted columns of the portico. Blood and fur and feces and urine covered the portico, but it was the terror-scarred, lifeless eyes and gaping mouths of the lambs that cut deep. Detective Gregus *felt* that deep cut. Detective Linda Barnes *did not*. In some dark corner of her inwardness, she was feeling euphoric. The whole macabre scene filled her with delight. She felt as if she were breathing fresh air after fighting her way up from the depths of the ocean to the water's surface. When she turned back to Gregus, she astutely hid the euphoria.

"This is not some random prank by a bunch of teenage misfits," said Gregus. "This is methodic and purposeful."

"You think this is the work of a satanic cult?" asked Barnes.

Gregus rubbed his forehead. His skin was red and flaky. "I don't know. But I know somebody who can tell us. Dr. James Knox. He taught at Hopkins. He's a demonologist."

Barnes laughed. "A what? A dermatologist?"

"This ain't funny, Barnes." Gregus turned away momentarily. He felt like punching Barnes in the face. "Dr. Knox is a Ph.D., not an M.D. He's a specialist in the occult. I met him a few years ago in the emergency room at Mercy Hospital. His wife was badly beaten by a bunch of thugs and left for dead. I worked the case, and we became friends."

Barnes smirked. *Big fucking deal*, she thought. Then suddenly, a wave of compassion surged up within her. She thought she was going to puke. She turned away and walked to the top of the portico steps. Her head swam uneasily with vertigo. *My God,* she thought, *what's happening to me?* She turned back to the portico and saw the grisly scene before her as if for the first time.

"What the fuck is wrong with you, Barnes?" Gregus said impatiently.

Barnes swallowed hard. "Mark, I want to visit Dr. Knox with you. I want to understand what happened here."

Gregus shrugged his shoulders. "Are you going act like a cop or an asshole? I'm not subjecting Knox to you if you're going act like an asshole."

Barnes took a deep breath. "I'll be a cop."

Ten minutes later, Barnes pulled off the road and coasted into an abandoned parking lot at the corner of St. Paul and Preston Streets. She opened the driver's side door, hastily leaned out, and puked on the black asphalt. An otherworldly stench rose like steam from the yellow-green bile splattered beneath her. "Oh, God, help me," she said. "Please help me."

53

Dr. James Knox was sixty years old. His wife of thirty years had died due to complications from internal bleeding two weeks after her beating. He was never technically on the staff at the Hopkins Homewood campus, but rather had been a visiting professor for one semester from Yale. When he entered the lobby at the Belvedere Hotel, Detectives Gregus and Barnes were waiting for him.

Gregus shook the hand of Dr. Knox with an almost exaggerated reverence. "Jim, it's so good to see you. I appreciate your coming all the way from New Haven."

Dr Knox stood tall, about six feet three, with fat legs supporting his rotund torso. Wisps of white hair garnished his large head, and piercing, blue eyes peered out beneath bushy, white eyebrows. He shook the detective's hand in silence, but his sparkling eyes and warm smile spoke volumes. When he was introduced to Barnes, his eyes emptied a bright light into hers. Even with that kind of illumination, he did not see what was there.

The two detectives and Dr. Knox sat in overstuffed wing chairs around an antique coffee table in the John Eager Howard Room. Several well-coiffed patrons lingered at nearby tables and the bar with drinks and hors d'oeuvres. The fragrance of expensive perfume and aftershave hung in the air. After Dr. Knox ordered dry gin martinis all around, the three interlocutors bantered easily about the unpredictable Baltimore weather. Then things turned serious.

"The portico of the basilica looked like a bloodbath," said Gregus desperately. "The mutilated carcasses of lambs were strung on metal wires around the ten columns. It looked to me like the work of a satanic cult."

Dr. Knox sipped his martini with uncanny reverence. He gazed with pleasure at the surroundings of the John Eager Howard Room. Large windows were covered with heavy, ornate drapes which, if opened, would draw one's gaze out to the busyness of Eager Street. Twenty-foot ceilings, adorned with fresco paintings of cherubs in varied states of repose, gave one the sense of openness and possibility. The thick Persian rugs beneath one's feet provided an anchor of security. And finally, the expansive oak bar, lined with libations, beckoned the soul to be soothed and the mind to open to thoughts heretofore bridled.

"The Basilica of the Assumption was the first Roman Catholic cathedral in the United States. As such, it was the throne of the first Roman Catholic diocese in America. I agree with you, Mark. To target this particular church is not a coincidence." Dr. Knox glanced at a beautiful woman sitting at a nearby table. His hands methodically swiveled his martini glass back and forth. "The lambs are a symbol of the innocent flock that the Catholics supposedly guide and protect. Again, I agree with you. It appears to be the work of a satanic cult."

Detective Gregus felt the effects of his martini at both of his throbbing temples. A warm fuzziness enveloped his brain. "I'm not sure what to do. This kind of thing is rare in Baltimore. I'm looking for guidance."

Dr. Knox raised his empty glass. "I suggest we order another round of martinis."

Detective Linda Barnes had been silent up to this point. Drinking gin martinis agreed with her. Talking was not particularly essential. But finally, she spoke: "I'm more interested in the psychology behind the desecration. What exactly motivates a group of people to do something like this?"

Dr. Knox flagged down a waitress and ordered another round of drinks. Appearing satisfied that more martinis were imminent, he considered Barnes' question. "Ah, motivation! A hard thing to grasp. If the desecration is a purely random act by a crew of misguided joy-riders, then the motivation could be anything from utter boredom to testosterone run amok." Dr. Knox stared at the cleavage-laden beauty close by. His lips buzzed with the residue of gin anesthesia. "If, on the other hand, this is the work of the devil, then we are dealing with possession."

Barnes shook her head and took a deep breath. Somewhere deep inside she heard a voice: *Ah, now we get to something interesting!* "Can you elaborate? Are you serious when you say the devil possesses people?"

Dr. Knox smiled, showing two rows of brown, stained teeth betraying his fondness for cigars. "What I am about to tell you is not a particularly accepted theory among the traditional intelligentsia of the twentieth-century theological community." Dr. Knox paused and glanced once again at the buxom beauty at the adjacent table. He could feel some ancient buzzing deep in his loins. "Possession is as old as mankind. It is, in fact, what moves the world. All of us are possessed. Possessed by the power of God. Nothing moves without that power."

Dr. Knox gently rubbed the curvature of his gigantic belly. "Don't get all caught up with this word *God*. When I say God, I simply mean the supreme reality that put the cosmos into motion and keeps it going." Dr. Knox peered down at his belly and watched it heave up and down as he breathed. He seemed very proud of his prodigious girth. "What is hard for the intellect to grasp is the utter lack of free will that exists in the universe. I'm completely serious when I say that God is moving us around like puppets."

Dr. Knox felt saliva bubbling in his mouth as he saw a nipple of the buxom beauty appear at the crest of her blouse's plunging neckline. "It may seem strange, but even what we call the work of the devil is

God's work. There is no other force in the universe."

The fresh martinis arrived to everyone's delight. Linda Barnes smiled like a clown worked by a crafty ventriloquist. *What the fuck is wrong with me?* she thought. "So you're saying that both good and evil are the products of the same force?"

Dr. Knox took a deep breath as he watched the nipple-revealing goddess leave the John Eager Howard Room under God's power. His heart beat a little slower at the realization of his loss. "Yes, you are quite right. But this doesn't mean we should ignore our instincts. If we feel moved to combat the evil, we should do it with great resolve. That's what God wants us to do."

Linda Barnes felt a dizzy divide beneath her breastbone as she sipped her martini. There is something about the juniper berry that distinguishes gin from all other intoxicants: if there is a break or split in one's inwardness, the berry tends to intensify the chasm. "Dr. Knox, is it possible for one person to be moved by both good and evil at the same time?"

Dr. Knox eased back in his chair. His eyes took on a wild excitement. "Oh, yes, Detective. Most certainly." The good doctor gulped the last of his martini. "The potential for both good and evil is present in everyone. But for most of us, one force or the other dominates." Dr. Knox looked about for the waitress. He wanted another martini. "To tell you the truth, it is those who are caught in the middle that I really feel sorry for. They are literally split apart inside. At some point, something has to give."

A coughing fit, caused by a piece of martini olive grazing his windpipe, suddenly seized Detective Gregus. After making quite a scene—enunciated by guttural hacking—he caught his breath and swallowed carefully. "I didn't know you were a mystic, Jim. All this time I thought you were nothing more than a wooly-headed scholar."

Doctor Knox smiled sheepishly. "I ain't no mystic. That's something altogether different. I do have a guru, though. And I trust him implicitly. I believe what he tells me. I'm just repeating what he knows to be true."

"What's this guru's name?" asked Barnes. Both parts of her wanted to know. For different reasons.

"His name is Sri Peche. He lives in India. When he looks into your eyes, he sees all the way to the bottom of your soul. There's nowhere to hide." Dr Knox breathed heavily. "I wouldn't want that kind of vision. Too much responsibility comes with that kind of deep insight." Dr. Knox chuckled. "Hell, the devil himself could be sitting in this room, and I wouldn't even know it."

How right you are, thought Barnes. She stared pensively at a portrait, mounted over the fireplace, of an evil-looking canine. "So what's the prognosis for recovery? For someone possessed?" Barnes frightened herself with the question. It seemed to come out of nowhere.

"I really don't know," said Dr. Knox. "That too would be in God's hands."

Detective Mark Gregus shrugged his shoulders. "Let's get back to the task at hand." He stared hopefully at Dr. Knox. "What do we do? We have no witnesses to the desecration. We have no leads of any kind."

Dr Knox raised his bushy eyebrows. "I wish I could be of more help, Mark. I did a little research before coming to see you. There are no recognized satanic cults here in Baltimore. There are some fringe-group wackos that fancy themselves as demonic, but I don't see them as the culprits. They couldn't pull off something this elaborate. Something foul is certainly afoot, but I can't point you toward anyone in particular. I'm sorry."

Detective Gregus loosened his blue and gold striped tie and unbuttoned the collar of his white oxford shirt. "I guess there's only one thing to do," he said, chuckling. "Order more martinis."

54

The black Jeep pulled to a slow stop in front of Father Byron's country hermitage. Linda Barnes looked into the rearview mirror. There she was. A forty-two-year-old, burned-out cop. No husband. No children. Not many friends to speak of.

Tap...tap...tap...Barnes jumped, startled by the knock on the car window. Rolling it down, she felt a dark, cold, dampness engulf her in sudden sadness. A bitterness cascaded across her tongue.

"Are you okay?" Father Byron asked, smelling pleasantly of pipe tobacco.

"Not really." Barnes felt like getting the hell out of there but fought back the compulsion.

Byron stepped back from the car. "Come on in. We'll get something warm to drink."

The two walked to the house together. Silence in the chill of the night. Just before the doorway, they searched for one another—hands met and held fast in the uncertainty of it all.

Byron's study. A mystical chamber. Pervaded by the smoke of pipe tobacco. Heavy, aromatic stillness. A pleasant yellow glow from a floor lamp, the shade draped with some exotic multicolored Asian silk. They drank Turkish coffee and ouzo in silence.

Byron's dark eyes were like mysterious pools of blackness. "So what kind of large cat has your tongue tonight?"

Linda Barnes looked away, fighting back tears of self-loathing. She feigned a smile. "I guess you're seeing the real me tonight."

Byron smiled calmly. "Is that so? Tonight you show sadness, regret, and fatigue. Tomorrow something will happen, and you'll feel lighthearted. Maybe even happy. Which person is the real you?" Byron slowly sipped his ouzo. "The real problem with our search for identity is that the object of our search is an illusion. We don't have a permanent identity. Believe me, once you give up *that* quest, life becomes much more tolerable."

Barnes. Silent. Indrawn. Self-imploding.

Byron held her hand. "All right. Let's start here and now. I'll ask questions, you give answers. I want you to *listen* to your answers just as I listen to them. I think you'll learn something."

Barnes squeezed Byron's hand ever so slightly. "All right."

"Why are you a cop? And why homicide?"

Barnes took a deep breath. *I don't want to go there. Ah, what the hell!* "It just happened, I guess. A nine-to-five office job never much interested me. So when I got out of college, I applied to the police academy. After I got on my feet, I worked undercover in narcotics for a few years. Did pretty well. They rewarded me with a detective's shield. I'm only the third female homicide detective to hold the position in Baltimore City."

"I don't doubt it."

"It took a while for the guys to accept me. But I think I've finally gained their respect."

Byron filled her glass with ouzo. "So now you're a member of the club?"

Barnes rubbed her tired eyes with a light touch of her fingertips. "I guess what's really happened is that I've become as cold and hard as they are. I'm afraid it's not a pretty picture. I have grave doubts about myself."

Byron locked his eyes on hers, intuiting her pain. "Elaborate, please."

I don't like where this is going, she thought. "You know, I really don't want to talk about this."

Byron sipped his ouzo, and the taste of licorice danced across his lips. "I want you to keep going. You need to listen to yourself."

Barnes. Shadows of weariness around the eyes and mouth. "I guess what I really doubt is my ability to be a whole person. My ability to..." Palpable silence. Making the heart skip. "I don't know what to do."

Dick gently touched her cheek with the back of his hand. "You're doing fine."

Linda shook her head. "Don't you see? I don't like who I am. I'm a mess. I don't think I can do what I want to do."

"What is it you want to do?"

Linda's eyes filled with shards of clear ice. No tears here. "I want some semblance of normalcy." Silence. She swallowed hard. "Hell, I guess I just want what everyone wants." Linda placed her glass of ouzo firmly on the coffee table. "Hell, I don't know what I'm saying."

Byron smiled gently and kindly shrugged his shoulders.

"My life is so fucked up. All I see is death and mutilated bodies and suffering families. That's the business I'm in. Working in homicide is like taking a contract out on your own sanity. You try to be strong. But there's only so much suffering you can take. And then you just go numb. I'm just not sure I have the capacity to live in any kind of healthy way. When you really think about it, what do I have to offer?"

Linda Barnes looked at Byron. He had such sad eyes. Eyes that perhaps had seen too much. Or maybe they were just mirrors reflecting her own image. "And what is *love*, anyway? What is *that* all about?" Linda Barnes dropped her head in sadness and confusion. *Why am I bringing that shit up?*

"Love is not something you can control," Byron said. "It's either there or it isn't. It doesn't matter whether you want it or not. It just surfaces and it's there. I really believe it comes when we're ready for it, not before."

Linda sadly rolled her eyes.

Byron, speaking softly, said, "Love is a gift. It's a product of grace. It just comes into our hearts. There are some rare people, the saints and mystics, who are the embodiment of love. They have love in their hearts always. But I think most of us just have to wait. Some of us live a lifetime without love, just waiting."

Linda stared hopelessly into her glass of ouzo. "I'm afraid of love coming into my life. Because if it did, I'd just screw it up."

Byron leaned back in his chair. His eyes were focused on something not spatial. "Linda, love is the least understood dimension of our existence. At its deepest, it is not a romantic emotion at all. Love rises up when wisdom and compassion flower simultaneously. When wisdom and compassion balance one another like the two wings of a bird in flight, loves shines forth like a beacon of hope."

Barnes felt a heavy sadness weigh on her slouching shoulders. "You speak beautiful words. But I'm afraid there's no poetry in *my* life. If love comes to me, it won't stay long."

Byron smiled sadly. "You may be right. But why do you care how long it stays? Everything in this cosmos is subject to coming and going. You must learn to trust nature, trust life, and move with it. It serves no purpose to resist. Life will tear you to pieces if you don't befriend it. Allow yourself to go wherever it takes you. Don't pick and choose. Just give your best effort to whatever moves you."

"But, Dick, I feel like I have no strength. There's nothing left inside."

"That's a fallacy. You think you have no strength because there's nothing left inside you. The real reason you have no strength is because you have too much inside you. Your thoughts, feelings, and emotions are choking your strength like weeds choking the life out of a garden. If you empty yourself completely of all your selfish involvement, the pure energy of life will rush into you and carry you along effortlessly."

Linda sat quietly, retreating deep within herself, her ears burning. *I'm not well,* she thought. "I'm overwhelmed. Let's talk about something else."

Byron raised his glass of ouzo respectfully. "All right. I think we've dressed your wounds enough for tonight."

Linda drained her glass of ouzo. "I have a question to ask you. How can you be a priest when you've lost your parish and your faith in Catholicism?"

Dick smiled. "Now we enter my closet of dirty laundry. I'm still a priest because it's safe to be a priest."

"What do you mean by 'safe'?"

"Well, I have the opportunity from time to time to help people. I enjoy that. I also have the leisure to read and write and think. And I like that. But most of all, being a priest without a parish means being left alone. I like the solitude. It's safe."

"It sounds to me like you're lazy."

Dick smiled playfully. "Yes, I'm lazy. But I'll tell you something. Without solitude, I don't think I could possibly have come to understand anything."

"Like what?"

The priest leaned close to her and whispered, "I understand that there is nothing to understand."

Barnes rolled her eyes. "Give me a break."

Byron smiled and thoughtfully stroked his beard. "Gertrude Stein put it this way: *There ain't no answer. There ain't going to be any answer. There never has been an answer. That's the answer.*"

"What if I said that's a clever philosophical cop-out?"

"Some might think so. And that's okay. I have no desire to convince anybody of anything. What's interesting to me is that so many of the really deep thinkers, whether they are from the East or the West, seem to end up embracing this paradox. Socrates, Aquinas, Nietzsche, Heidegger, Wittgenstein, Einstein, Heisenberg—they all, in their own ways, came to the marvelous understanding that there really is nothing to understand. The story of life is an ongoing mystery. A mystery to engage in and endure. That's all."

Byron continued: "And then, of course, there are the great seers of the East—the Buddha and Lao Tzu and Ramana Maharshi. They all had one simple insight: *Be who you are. You cannot be other than you are.* All life changes when this one simple insight is realized."

Linda smirked, unconvinced. "If there's nothing to understand, why do we go to all the effort to educate ourselves?"

"Ah, but that's the point. Education and understanding, or perhaps I should say education and wisdom, are two different things. We need to be educated. We need to know how to read and write, do mathematics, learn about history and science. All of that is necessary to get along with the practicalities of life. But wisdom, now that's something else. Wisdom is about seeing into the true nature of things, seeing what is right there in front of you without any distortion or prejudice. The only way you can do that is to really understand that you know nothing. If you think you know something, then that something clouds or distorts your perception. You can't possibly see clearly. So once you know there's nothing to know, the mind games stop, and life opens up to you for the first time. Then you come to feel what natural spontaneity is."

Linda peered at the priest through eyelids heavy with the burden of exhaustion. "I'm afraid you're going to have to run these ideas by me many times before I really get it."

"It will be my pleasure."

Linda gently rubbed her eyes. "I want to know why you lost your parish."

Byron smiled impishly. "It's really quite simple. I didn't say the things the congregation wanted to hear."

"Like what?"

"Most of it centered around the Vietnam War. It wasn't that I took the side of the protestors; it was simply that I understood what they were doing and was sympathetic to their cause. I also understood and was sympathetic to our military leaders. What my parish couldn't understand was how I didn't take sides—or maybe it was how I could see both sides."

"So the people complained to the Catholic hierarchy?"

"Yes. They drummed me out. Actually, I can't complain. The local archbishop told me to stay out of the way and mind my own business. So that's what I've done."

"It sounds like you're freeloading, living off the Catholic Church that you no longer believe in." A chill spiraled up Linda's spine. She could have sworn the already dark eyes of the priest became a shade darker.

The priest rose from his chair, walked to the window, and stood with his back to her. "You're right. I am freeloading. But, believe me, I paid a price for this opportunity." He turned and looked at her. She saw what looked like a ghost. "The reason the Catholics didn't excommunicate me was because I was willing to do their dirty jobs for them."

"What dirty jobs?" Linda leaned back in her chair, bracing herself for what was to come.

"I've never told a soul outside the Church what I'm about to tell you." Silence. Silence as hard as the frozen tundra. "I did exorcisms. Three of them. One in Mexico, one in Uruguay, one in Bali. The one in Bali nearly killed me. I didn't speak for a year after that one."

Linda leaned forward in her chair. "Oh, my God. I didn't know exorcisms happened anymore."

The priest moved away from the window and returned to his chair. His voice was just above a whisper. "Now they pretty much leave me alone. I've been blessed with a great opportunity—the opportunity of leisure. That opportunity I have not wasted."

Linda Barnes felt an uneasy mixture of excitement and impending doom. "Dick, you don't have to talk about the exorcisms if you don't want to, but it does interest me. Are these people really possessed by demons, or are we talking about some extreme form of psychosis?"

The dark eyes of the priest flickered with some internal light. "Demons. No doubt about it. More often than not, the demons rise up in the vulnerable. The children. The elderly. And sometimes, they inhabit the powerful personalities. These are the ones that do the most destruction. To recognize the existence of demons was the last and final truth I had to accept and digest as a man of God."

Linda Barnes scratched at her *burning* left ear. *Pointy. Odd.* "And who combats these evil forces? Batman and Robin?"

Byron's eyes flashed a humorless stare. "You'd be surprised at how it works. Anyone can be called upon to serve the force of goodness. Make no mistake about it: The forces of good and evil are in perfect balance. For every demon that rises up, there is an angel to combat it. The demons and angels work through us. We are their instruments."

Linda silently shook her head. Her eyes told him to continue.

"All of this, everything you see and hear and touch and think, is nothing but the manifestation of God. All that is good, all that is evil. There is nothing but God. Extreme forms of goodness we call miracles. Extreme forms of evil we call horrors. We can understand neither. Angels exist and so do demons. Again, we can understand neither. When the angels and the miracles appear, we feel that God is close by. When the demons and horrors appear, we feel that God has abandoned us. What we fail to realize is that the demon is no less God than the angel. If you try to understand this rationally, in terms of good and evil, or right and wrong, it can't be digested. The mind is simply not capable of grasping it."

Linda smirked. "Well, I certainly don't understand it."

"Oh, but you do. What do you think is going on out there in the streets, the very streets you try to keep safe? Those horrors you clean up after are committed by the demons that rise up within us. It's not unlike a tornado or tempest. Things are somewhat normal, maybe even calm, and then something happens, and the winds start to whip. The next thing you know, there is a raging torrent of destruction. The same thing happens within a human being. The psychic storm is the demon raising its head. We can easily accept the weather storm as the *power of God*, but it is not so easy to accept the psychic storm that way. But, truly, there is no difference."

Linda Barnes stared into the eyes of the priest. It felt as if she were straining to see the top of a very high mountain.

"There is a paradox in knowing the truth of this," said Byron. "When you fully digest that God is behind it all, it shatters your mind. It doesn't just feel like death, it is death. The individual personality is no longer there."

Linda shook her head, bewildered. "Is there anything left?"

"Yes. Peace. Peace comes when there is total, unconditional surrender to whatever happens."

"The exorcisms brought you to this point?"

"Yes. They tore me apart. They eliminated me."

Linda looked at him quizzically. "Would you have it any other way?"

"No. It was my destiny."

The room became uneasily silent, like the aftermath of a deafening blow to the head.

Linda Barnes didn't want to know anything more about destiny. "Tell me more about the leisure and solitude you enjoy."

The priest smiled. "The way I see it, I've slipped between the cracks. But that's part of the blessing. I didn't ask for the Church to take away my parish. I didn't ask for leisure and solitude. It just came to me. And if or when it's taken away, I know something will come in its place. That's the way life is. Coming and going, coming and going. I no longer worry about such things. I really believe that life knows what it's doing."

"This may sound pedestrian, but what do you do for money?"

"That, too, just seems to come. I still get a little money from the Catholics. And I make a little writing essays for philosophical and religious journals. But oddly enough, most of my money comes from benefactors—people I've helped. At one time I did something to keep them going, and now they are kind enough to keep me going."

Linda shook her head and took a deep breath. "What are we doing together, Dick? This is too damn confusing."

Dick sat quietly, stroking his beard. "It's only confusing if you demand to understand it. If you make no demands, it just is what it is."

"But what is it?"

"All I can say is that life has brought us together. It's for sure neither of us asked for this. But here we are. And you know what?"

"What?"

"We really can't break free until life decides to release us. I guess you could say we're stuck with one another—for better or for worse."

Linda sat quietly, her ears burning. A bitter taste in her mouth. "Which do you think it is?" she asked. Her voice, husky and hardly recognizable.

"For better or for worse?"

Byron, as serene as a statue of the Buddha, his dark eyes gazing out at the future, said, "Only time will tell."

55

Oh, the sad, sad, fickle finger of fate. As Father Byron prepares for bed, he is thinking of Linda Barnes. The thoughts are uncomfortably engulfed by dark shadows. He knows what's coming.

As for Ms. Barnes, she is, at this moment, an expression of feral, sensual intensity. She is tasting blood. The blood of a baby rabbit. A baby rabbit that she has intentionally hit with her car. She is off the road now. Down by Loch Raven Reservoir. The blood is warm and sweet in her mouth. The blood comes from the neck of the lifeless creature. In the moonlight, the ears of Linda Barnes protrude up through her hair. Pointy. Reddish. Odd.

56

Six Months Later

"I'm leaving the priesthood."

"You're serious, aren't you?" asked Father Mark Welch.

"Yeah, I am."

Father Welch rose from his straight-backed, wooden chair and toddled out of the less-than-tiny efficiency kitchen. His gray hair thinned out over the crown of his head, revealing a huge forehead below. It looked as if his squat body were doing all it could to support his abundant forehead.

Father Welch walked, with a little skip in his gait, to a mahogany hutch in the corner of his small room at the monastery. He opened the lower door of the hutch and produced a bottle with an elaborate blue and silver label. "This calls for the Romana Sambuca." His deep-set, dark eyes looked lost beneath his monstrous forehead.

Byron smiled. "Ah, the sambuca. We must be about to embark on a very serious conversation."

Father Welch placed the bottle on the retro-1950s Formica kitchen table and retrieved two shot glasses from the sink. "The fact that you have come to this precipice doesn't surprise me," said Father Welch as he rinsed out the shot glasses.

Father Byron smiled as he watched his dear friend ease himself back into his chair. Byron chuckled to himself as he thought, *Old Mark always resorts to the sambuca when the going gets tough.*

Father Welch poured the sambuca into the shot glasses. "Let's not forget the *chicchi di caffè*." The good father leaned down, opened the portable fridge sitting on the floor, and retrieved a plastic bag filled with coffee beans. He plopped three into each glass. "The first coffee bean promises you health, the second promises you wealth, the third promises you happiness. *Salute!*" he said, and the two priests ceremoniously kicked back the libation.

Father Byron gazed at the faded writing on his shot glass: *St. Bernard Oyster Roast 1989*. He refilled the glasses and leaned back in his chair. He felt the pleasant sting of licorice on his lips. "Well, Mark, it's really quite simple. I'm tired of being a sham priest. It's unbecoming."

Father Welch smiled and shook his huge head. "Ah, we're all shams for Jesus. I don't see any stalwart examples of Christ around here or anywhere else for that matter. So don't try to make me feel sorry for you."

Father Byron smirked. "Jeeez, and I thought you were going to show me some compassion. Go figure!"

Father Welch carefully leaned forward. His forehead glistened in the soft light of the efficiency kitchen. Dark ridges beneath his eyes gave notice of severe exhaustion. "Seriously, Dick, if someone came to me and asked me to point them toward the most spiritually advanced person I know, I'd send them to you." A pregnant pause. "In fact, I *have* sent them to you."

Father Welch sipped the licorice-flavored nectar. "I know you don't believe in the Church. But what the hell? In this day and age, when we're spiritually bankrupt, I don't think it matters. What's important is the wisdom you have to offer. That's what matters."

"I can still give the wisdom. I just don't want to use the Christian trappings any longer. It worked fine for a while, but now things have changed."

"Really?" asked Father Welch. "How so?"

"There's a woman. I'm drawn to her and she to me."

Father Welch shrugged his shoulders and rolled his eyes. "It happens, Dick. Believe me, it will pass. Just let it pass by."

Father Byron smiled impishly. "Oh, my dear friend, it's not what you think. The fact that we're drawn together does not necessarily imply that happiness lies ahead. You know me better than that. I've never put much stock in my own happiness."

Father Welch nodded in acknowledgement of the living truth sitting before him. "So what's this about, then?"

Shadows of seriousness fell over Father Byron's face. "It looks like I've been called upon, once again, to do some of God's dirty work. The woman in question is possessed. The only way I can help her is to get close to her. The priestly garb has to go. It's the right thing to do."

Father Welch despondently shook his head. He felt as if he were a kite with no wind beneath it. "Oh, my. I must tell you this upsets me. I don't know how many more of these dirty jobs you have in you."

"Mark, you know how it happens with me. It's not like I have a choice in the matter. There really is no entity named Dick Byron inhabiting this body. God just picks up this sack of skin and bones and uses it as he wishes." Father Byron sadly stared at his old friend. "I'm not trying to upset you. You must know that. I'm just giving you fair warning."

Father Welch took a deep breath. "Does the woman know what's going on? Is she aware that she's possessed?"

"She knows something is wrong. She has said as much." Father Byron licked a drop of sambuca from his lower lip. "I'm just going to allow myself to be moved by the divine energy. If it's in the stars that I help her, so be it."

Father Welch leaned back in his chair, his huge forehead majestically imposing itself. "I have never really understood who you are. My lot in life is to be a simple Catholic priest. Your lot is something quite unfathomable to me."

Father Byron smiled at his long-time friend. "I have always envied you. A simple Catholic priest. It must be rather pleasant."

Father Welch forced a smile. "Yeah. It is rather pleasant."

Father Byron smiled mischievously and turned up his nose like a dilettante. "One only needs to cast a glance at your regal forehead to know you are a simple man of scholarship and letters. No riff-raff in your life. Books, a quill writing pen, and the open air of solitude. It is true, my friend, I envy you."

Father Welch smiled sheepishly. "I must tell you, Dick, I've always felt grateful that I was not chosen to go down your priestly path. It's just not in my nature."

"That's the beauty of the priesthood. God gives us the work that *does* fit our nature. What I'm called to do may seem foreign to you, but to me it's literally illuminating. I feel God's presence all the time. It's like a firm but gentle push that makes me do what I do." Father Byron thoughtfully stroked his beard. "Remember, I'm not sent on these dirty missions that often. For the most part, I live the contemplative life just as you do."

Father Welch slugged down his sambuca. "Do you remember the woman I sent to you last fall? Her name was Lisa Browning."

Father Byron leaned forward in thoughtful repose. "Oh, yes, I remember her. Why do you ask?"

"I read about her death in the newspaper. To be honest, I didn't want to know what happened between the two of you. That's part of being a simple Catholic priest. Just mind the immediate flock. Don't get too involved outside the domain."

Father Byron slowly wiped at his lips with the back of his left hand. "Lisa Browning was a remarkable woman. Extremely courageous. She was psychic, you know. She was receiving messages from beyond. Messages were coming to her in dreams as well as in the waking state. Hell, Mark, she even felt the presence of the ghosts from St. James Parish."

Father Welch smacked his lips as he peered at Byron through squinting eyes. "What happened, Dick? Why was she murdered?"

"The murder was never solved. There was a suspect but no substantial incriminating evidence." Byron shrugged his shoulders. "The cops call this type of case a 'red ball.'"

Father Welch smiled halfheartedly. "We're all here doing God's work. My work is simple but necessary. Your work is anything but simple. And I sometimes wonder if it's necessary."

Byron gazed at Father Welch with a far-off look. "To be sure, it is necessary. I wouldn't be driven to do it otherwise."

Father Welch haplessly shook his massive head. "Dick, forgive me. I had no good reason to say that, other than my obvious lack of understanding. If you wish to take the time to explain it to an old,

191

fuzzy-headed priest with little imagination, I'd be grateful."

"Take a walk with me," Byron said, as he stood up and stretched his legs.

57

The two priests walked contemplatively across the campus of St. Mary's Seminary. The summer evening sparkled with fireflies arching their way through alternating spaces of darkness and moonlight.

"The full moon literally opens your mind. Did you know that?" said Byron.

"It wouldn't surprise me," said Father Welch. "The full moon seems to spur mental and emotional upheavals like no other recurring natural phenomenon."

Byron laughed knowingly. "You no longer sound like some simple Catholic priest. I think this charade you put forth is like an experienced hustler going in for the kill at a poker table."

"Pay me no mind, Dick." Father Welch scratched at the back of his neck. His skin felt unpleasantly clammy. "Tell me more about this woman who's entered your life with such a splash."

The two men stopped under a tall, gray, metallic lamppost. An insistent electric buzz hissed away at them from above. They stood in silence in their gray sweat suits and white running shoes. The grass beneath their feet smelled of honey and sassafras.

"The woman I'm drawn to is a homicide detective," said Byron. "She was working the Lisa Browning case." Byron pointed to the full moon above. "That bright little rascal up there was really moving the tides to bring the two of us together."

The two priests walked across the monastery courtyard in silence and made themselves comfortable on a wooden bench next to a fragrant yellow rosebush.

Father Byron inhaled the majesty of the evening. "The detective's name is Linda Barnes. I sensed the attraction between us the moment we met." Byron gently brushed the grass beneath the bench with his running shoe. "Linda and I never would have met had Lisa Browning's quiet attempt at suicide not been redirected by a madman."

Father Welch quizzically squinted his eyes. "Is that why Lisa was seeking your counsel? Because she was considering suicide?"

Byron leaned down and picked a yellow rose petal off the ground. "Yes. But her mind was already made up. She just wanted my assistance with the aftermath."

Byron contemplated the petal. "Mark, Lisa was a lot like this simple yellow rose petal. She appeared here on earth and bloomed. Her life was one of graceful giving. And then the energy keeping her here dissipated, and she broke free. Like this rose petal, she bloomed beautifully and separated from the vine at precisely the right time."

Byron dropped the petal and watched it fall gently to the ground. "Do you remember the insight of Nietzsche? He said we need to die at the right time. That's what Lisa was doing—dying at the right time."

Byron looked out into the evening blackness. "Lisa had the extraordinary blessing of seeing clearly into her own destiny without fear or regret. What none of us saw coming was the means of actualizing that destiny."

Father Welch slowly raised himself from the bench. The letters spelling *Georgetown* blazed across his sweatshirt in the yellow moonlight. "Let's go have a beer. Let's go to the Swallow at the Hollow."

Byron looked up at his friend. "Yeah, let's go to the Swallow."

58

"The first time I was aware of the ghosts was in Milan. I was a young priest. Full of enthusiasm. Ready to share the joys of Catholicism with the world." Byron took a deep breath and dismissively shook his head. "Little did I know." Byron took a sip of Bass Ale and relished the bitter sting it left on his lips.

It was after midnight. The Swallow at the Hollow was safe harbor to quiet drinkers looking for some temporary anchor in the windblown sea of life. Father Welch stared at Byron with pursed lips. He raised his furry eyebrows as a sign for Byron to continue.

"At any rate, I was in the Church of Santa Maria delle Gràzie. It was sometime after midnight. One of the old monks watching over the place allowed me access to the refectory. I sat there by myself, gazing at Leonardo's *Last Supper* by candlelight."

Byron smiled wistfully. "I was trying to take in the painting and all it stood for. I was trying to have some special vision, as if only Catholic priests could be privy to such things. The problem was that I was trying to see it with my intellect. I wanted to penetrate its mystery with the power of my own reason."

Byron smirked knowingly. "What a fool I was. It wasn't until I stopped *trying* to see the painting and simply allowed it to speak to me that it all became clear. Suddenly, a transparent, silver veil filtered down from above and completely enveloped the refectory. The veil transported the entire scene beyond space and time—and I was no longer alone. Jesus and his disciples and his betrayers were all there, sitting around me at one of the dining tables. The ghosts were eating in silence. Not a word was spoken. But they were all inescapably connected to Jesus. He was the thread that held them all together. Without that thread, the fabric of life would dramatically change!

"I knew then, by some strange flowering of intuition, the true meaning of Christ's death on the cross. The Christians try to play a game with the death of Christ. They say he died *for* us, that we now have a chance at redemption *because* he died *for* us. That kind of thinking is not only misleading, but also dangerous. When Jesus was nailed to the cross and left to die in agony, God was sending the world a very different message. That message, quite simply, is this: *In this life, anything can happen! Inexplicable goodness coexists with inexplicable evil. It's all part of the total drama. It's all to be endured.*"

Byron felt the chill of the beer glass against his fingertips. The smell of barley and hops filled his nose. "I knew then that there is nothing to escape. Christ did not die *for* us. He was simply *sacrificed*. The God-man was there one moment and gone the next. There's nothing to escape. *Everything and everyone will be sacrificed!* That is the price we pay for existing within space and time."

Byron slowly leaned back in his wobbly, wooden chair. He could feel himself delicately balanced on the two back legs. "The sacrifices are anything but random. They are all purposeful. They all deliver a message. And they all bring about strong waves of reactions. The reactions to the sacrifices are as important as the sacrifices themselves. The reactions move the drama along."

Byron stared across the tavern at a drunken young man feeling up his girlfriend in a corner booth. "The Buddha had the answer. It's the same answer that Christ gave, silently, on the cross. *Endure. Life is to be endured. The good comes and goes. Evil comes and goes. It all is to be endured.*" Byron wondered about the softness and warmth of the girl's breast. "A Hindu guru once told me that the important thing in life is to *get through it*, to somehow navigate the tight channel and make it through. Once we're through, our job is done."

Father Welch squinted as he cleaned his spectacles on a protruding fold of his sweatshirt. "So all the clever explanations of our philosophy and psychology are ultimately useless. Do you really mean that?"

Byron smiled. His sad, dark eyes reflected the yellow glow of the barroom. "Precisely. I'm not trying to be clever. There is no deeper meaning to life. The enlightened life is simply a matter of *endurance.* Ignorance is not endurance. Avoidance is not endurance. Fanaticism is not endurance. Endurance means swallowing all that life throws at you. Swallowing it and digesting it completely. And then continuing on with circumspection and dignity. Endurance means you live without absolute answers, and yet you do not wobble."

Byron looked around the barroom. Many sad, empty faces stared into glasses half-filled with magical libations. "Lisa Browning did not wobble. She knew what was going on. Her run on life was coming to an end. She gladly accepted it. It was all overlooked when she was murdered. That's the problem: the murder got all the attention. The goodness and wisdom expressed by Lisa were not digested. Both good and evil need to be digested. There can be no wisdom otherwise."

Father Welch rubbed his tired eyes with his stubby fingertips. "Let's head back, Dick."

The two priests paid the bill and left the tavern in silence. The silence continued throughout the forty-five-minute walk back to the monastery. The two men embraced in silence at the steps leading to Father Welch's rectory. Byron drove home in silence.

Early the next morning, Byron answered the phone in his kitchen. There was a long, gut-wrenching pause. "Thank you," Byron said dryly and hung up the phone.

Father Welch's body was found at 6:30 a.m. in the gutter at the corner of East Cold Spring Lane and Roland Avenue. He had been taking an early morning walk when an automobile struck him. The driver left the scene. There were no witnesses.

59

Detective Linda Barnes was sucking wind as she crouched down in the dark shadows of the alley, balancing herself cat-like on the balls of her feet. Her heart, pounding like a jackhammer, nearly blotted out the sound of police sirens filling the warm night air above her. "Come on, backup. Come on, backup," she whispered desperately to herself.

She held her gun up close to her chest as she listened intently for sounds of movement on the other side of the massive steel Dumpster. For two blocks, she had chased a street derelict wielding a monstrous .44 magnum before pinning him down in this dead-end alley in the one hundred block of Guilford Avenue. Her pulse throbbed at her temples as she replayed dodging two wildly fired shots from the magnum cannon. She had *never* been shot at before. She took it personally.

The stench from the rotting garbage overflowing the Dumpster made her gag with every breath. And in and out of the shadows moved the rats. Big, fat rats with red eyes and long, cord-like tails. The rats scurried about indiscriminately. After all, it was their home.

Barnes shielded herself against the back of the Dumpster and prepared to shoot. When she yelled out, her voice wavered. "I'm a police detective. I've got backup on the way. You're pinned down in this alley, and you're not getting out. It's to your advantage to drop your gun and give up *now*. When my backup gets here, it could get bloody."

Dark silence filled the dead-end Baltimore alley. A rat grazed Barnes' left ankle just as a drop of sweat cascaded down the bridge of her nose. None of it bothered her. None of it mattered.

"All right, motherfucker. Here's what we're going to do," Barnes shouted. Her voice was on automatic pilot. She wasn't sure what was going to come out next. "I want you to slide your gun out on the pavement where I can see it. *Do it! Now!*"

To her surprise, the haughty magnum slid across the open alleyway, clattering noisily to a halt about three feet in front of her. The gleaming silver cannon, lying on its side amidst the slop of garbage and disintegrating cobblestone, looked like some strange icon from an age no longer remembered.

"All right," Barnes shouted. "Now lie face down on the ground, with your arms and legs spread." Barnes was breathing in short, quick gulps of air, but her hands held her gun steady. "If you're not on the ground when I come around, I'll blow your fucking head off."

Like some feline creature accustomed to surviving in the wild, Barnes crept, stealthily, around the corner of the Dumpster. Keeping one eye riveted on the open space awaiting her next step, she carefully bowed down to secure the magnum. It was heavy and cold in her hand, like some evil weight trying to pull her down into the bowels of hell.

After a moment's consideration, she decided to situate the gun under the far side of the Dumpster, away from the derelict. When she placed the gun on the ground, she noticed how still the night had become and how the silence provided an opportunity for every sound to be heard with curious certitude. When the magnum touched the cobblestone floor of the alley, it echoed curiously. And when the echo subsided, the quiet filled her with fear. All she could hear now was the *absence* of police sirens. No backup was coming.

Detective Linda Barnes secured her weapon in both hands in front of her and made her way around the Dumpster. It was as if some force were pushing her with just the right velocity. She relaxed into the movement and turned the far corner of the Dumpster. First, she saw the shoes of the derelict. Old, tattered Converse All-Stars. The soles were wet and glistened with the slickness of moist garbage. As her eyes surveyed forward, she saw a tall, lean, white man, facedown, in gray sweatpants and a black T-shirt. His bald head was turned slightly to the side, and his mouth grimaced with discomfort. A white baseball cap lay next to his head. The red lettering across the front of the cap said *Bullets*.

"All right, my friend. So far, so good," said Barnes. She noticed her voice was unnecessarily loud. She took a deep breath. "Stay right where you are. I'm going to pat you down. If you fucking move an inch, I'll shoot you dead."

Barnes frisked the derelict and was relieved when she found no other weapons. Carefully holding her gun on him, she told him to crawl to the alley wall and sit with his back against it. Barnes backed up to the opposite wall, about twenty feet away, and sat on an abandoned, wooden crate.

Two beings, somehow brought together by the forces of nature, stared at one another in the dark shadows of the rat-infested alley.

What she saw was a lean man with clean-shaven head and face, dark, piercing eyes, and a pleasant smile. What she saw was a man with a relaxed and unhampered body. What she saw was a man exuding calm perspicacity. She was befuddled and unnerved by what she saw.

What he saw was a woman with short-cropped, brown hair, lazy, brown eyes with hints of amber sparkle, and a sad mouth with robust lips. What he saw was a body racked with tension. What he saw was a woman exuding inner conflict. He was not surprised by what he saw. It was as he expected it to be.

Linda Barnes held the gun on the derelict with utmost circumspection. She breathed heavily. "When I frisked you, I found no wallet. No keys. No money. What's your story, anyway?"

The derelict stared at Barnes in silence. When he finally spoke, his voice was soft and shimmering. "I have *no* story. The only story here is *yours*."

Barnes felt her insides turn. Her vocal chords seemed to lock up.

The derelict sat with his knees up against his chest. "May I stretch my legs out? I promise not to do anything stupid."

Barnes nodded her head.

The derelict slowly stretched his legs out before him. "Ah, that feels better." From out of the Dumpster, a trace of dark shadow filled the alley, and a rat landed between the derelict's legs.

Barnes jumped with a shutter. She held the gun tight but could not speak.

The rat sat like a cat between the legs of the derelict and stared up at him peacefully. "How are you, my friend?" the derelict said as he gently caressed the rat's head and ears. "Are you getting enough to eat? From the look of this alley, I would say you are." The rat made some prescient, whining sound that filtered through the warm night air like soft rain. "Now run along, my friend. I have business to attend to." The rat playfully sniffed at the derelict's hands and wandered off into the darkness.

The derelict now turned his full attention to Barnes. "We haven't much time. Allow me to simply say that we have been brought together for *your* benefit. It is *your* future that is at stake. You need not feel odd about speaking to me. And you need not explain anything. I already know everything about you. I am here as your ally. Use me for your own benefit."

As if waking from a dream of oppression, Barnes felt her vocal chords relax. Her head was swimming with dizziness, but soon some sense of balance reclaimed her. She took a deep breath and shook her head in bewilderment. "So what the hell are you? Some kind of angel?"

The derelict wistfully shrugged his shoulders. "Something like that." He gently touched the palm of his hand to his chest. "Please, use me for your benefit."

Barnes winced as a stabbing pain radiated through her breastbone. "I guess you know I haven't been feeling well lately." Her voice was deep and raspy. "Some would say I have a touch of the *devil* in me." Barnes' eyes opened wide and shot out a yellow, incandescent light. "I take distinct pleasure in bringing harm to others," she growled with satisfaction.

The derelict smiled, undisturbed. "I know all that. I told you, you don't have to explain." The derelict snapped his fingers, and a white dove appeared in the palm of his hand. The dove had deep blue eyes that sang a silent song of high altitudes and winter snow. "I am extending myself to you," said the derelict. "Please use me for your benefit."

Detective Linda Barnes felt her chest collapse. Whatever strength she had was being sucked out of her. Then some warm, inner light washed up from deep within her. When she spoke, her voice was soft and measured. "I don't know who I am. I don't know what to do. I am *completely* lost. Perhaps forever." Barnes sat silently, engulfed by the heat and putrid smells of the dead-end alley. Then she raised her head to the dark sky and saw the white dove circling high above her. The lights from the downtown harbor reflected off the wings of the dove like moonlight dancing on a serene lake. Then a glow spread out around the dove, and it froze in mid-flight like some gigantic, aboriginal hummingbird.

"Our time is short. How would you like to use me?" said the white dove.

Linda Barnes hypnotically rose to a standing position, her body stretching out to the sky. "Help me! For God's sake, help me!" Her body strained to reach the dove's awareness.

The white dove gently fluttered its wings as if in slow motion. *"Help is already here. It has been reaching out to you for some time now. You must decide whether or not to take its hand."*

Barnes looked down at her hands. One held her gun; the other was like an open question, waiting with expectation. "I don't know how to take its hand," Barnes said despondently.

"Who are you? Look deep within, and tell me what you see."

Detective Linda Barnes backed up against the alley wall. The wall supported her like the arms of a trusted lover. She spoke to the night sky as if in a trance. "I am split in two. I have two faces. One invisibly on top of the other. They shift at random." Barnes' chest heaved spasmodically. "I have two hearts. One invisibly on top of the other." She winced with inner pain. "My deepest heart has trouble surfacing."

*"Who **are** you?"* bellowed the white dove.

Linda Barnes slid to the alley floor, breathing heavily.

The white dove hovered over Linda Barnes like a giant, lace mesh, its wings expanding into infinity. *"Allow your deepest heart to show itself! Take the helping hand, and allow it to guide you!"*

Sometimes the darkness of night is black through and through. Nothing stirs. Everything stays in its place.

~

Linda Barnes winced as a pulsating awareness of her body washed over her. She felt a soreness cascade through her being from head to toe. It was as if she had been thrown against an unforgiving wall by some unexpected explosion.

She heard sounds of voices coming from somewhere above her. A lazy, idle chatter signaling conversations of familiarity. Her throat closed involuntarily, bracing itself against some foul, yellow smell. Jarred by a painful back spasm, she opened her eyes.

She lay in the early morning shadows of a gray, rusted-out Dumpster. She blinked and wondered where the hell she was. Then it all came back to her in a titanic rush. She felt for her gun. It was at her side. She got up on one knee and quickly surveyed the length of the alley. It was empty, save for the rotting garbage and a couple of banged-up, abandoned bicycles. She looked up and saw a few open windows above her. She could smell the drifting aroma of burnt toast cascading down the brick alley wall. She stared, with failing excitement, at the wall opposite her. No derelict.

She crept across the alley and crawled behind the Dumpster where she had left the .44 magnum. No magnum. Something seemed to be floating against the alley wall. A pure white feather. As pure as snow in the highest mountains.

60

Dick Byron shook open the maroon army blanket and allowed it to float gently to the sun-bleached, grassy ground. He sat cross-legged on the blanket and gazed, with a delicate mixture of fondness and reverence, at the headstone of Father Mark Welch. Father Welch was buried in the cemetery on the grounds of St. Mary's Church in Govans.

A warm breeze swirled in the sunshine and massaged Byron's bare face and arms. Byron opened his leather briefcase, a handmade beauty that he had picked up years ago in Venice, and drew out a bottle of Romana Sambuca and two shot glasses. He poured out two shots. He placed one on the headstone of Father Welch and slugged down the other one with a graceful whip of his arm. The anise-based alcohol stung his lips and reminded him of his last conversation with Father Welch at St Mary's Seminary two months earlier. He filled his glass again and placed it on the headstone next to Father Welch's glass. "Well, my dear friend, we meet once again under the guidance of this magnificent Italian libation."

Dick Byron closed his eyes and bowed his head and torso to the headstone of Father Welch. "I miss you," Byron whispered. "I miss our conversations. I thought, perhaps, that if I showed up with the sambuca, I could coax you out of the dream of death."

Byron laughed at himself good-naturedly and opened his eyes. Standing above him, on the other side of the headstone, was an old man. He had long, wild, electrified, white hair, much in the manner of Einstein. His face was chiseled long and narrow, and his crystal clear, blue eyes completely filled their deep, recessed sockets. Even on this warm summer day, he wore a tan London Fog raincoat. When the wind blew, the coat flapped as if there were no one inside.

"I see you're having a party with an old friend," the old man said. He majestically waved his drooping coat sleeve at the surrounding grounds. "Did you know that in the old parish records, this cemetery is referred to as *God's Acre?* It's true." The old man swiveled his head around in short, spasmodic jerks to take in the churchyard setting. "You won't see trees any prettier than these. We've got some big old red maples and some lindens and oaks. And then there are the tall evergreens." The old man shook his head in wonder. "Yep, *God's Acre.* That's what they call it."

The old man stared at the glasses of sambuca perched on the headstone of Father Welch. "I've had a few of those in my day. For some reason, it always seemed to loosen my tongue. And not without good results. I always spoke the truth under the influence of that kind spirit."

Byron suddenly felt himself shifting to one side of the blanket. He was as light as a feather. He gently patted the blanket. "Why don't you sit down and join me?"

The old man smiled. "Don't mind if I do."

In a non-temporal flash, the old man settled down next to Byron. The blue eyes of the old man hypnotized him. There was something familiar about them. Not the eyes themselves but what lay behind them.

Byron watched silently as the old man lifted the glass of sambuca from the headstone, closed his eyes, and slowly swallowed the spirit. His raincoat seemed to collapse to nothing as the air danced breezily under the canopy of warm summer radiance. The old man placed his glass back on the headstone and turned his attention to Byron. His blue eyes locked profoundly into the depths of Byron's own. "Thanks for coming, my friend. I have missed you as well."

EDWARD FOTHERINGILL

Byron felt himself take a deep, resourceful breath. It was as if someone from beyond were breathing through him. "Well, I'll be damned. You old son-of-a-gun. You've crossed over. You've crossed over, haven't you?" Byron felt the purity of bliss cascading through his mind and body.

The old man laughed. "Something like that. I'm only able to cross over because of you. Because you have one foot over here already, I can contact you. Otherwise, it would not be possible."

Byron couldn't stop smiling. His wide-open eyes stared at the spirit of Father Welch. "What's it like where you are? Is it as pleasant as I suspect?"

The old man closed his eyes in blissful repose. "It is really not describable in human terms. But if you insist, I would use three words to point to the experience: silence, stillness, and unity. It is fragmentation and separation that cause sound and movement. Here, there is none of that." The old man opened his eyes and considered Byron's face with devotion. "You have been right all this time. All your so-called mystical insights are right on the money. That's why you have one foot over here where I am."

Byron playfully squinted with a mixture of certitude and mischief. "Well, I'm certainly glad to have finally got you to see things my way!" After a moment's reflection, Byron turned serious. "It upset me how you left all of a sudden. I know it can happen that way, but the part of me that stands in this world still struggles with it."

The old man smiled wistfully. "Ah, don't worry about it. We don't have any control over it. You always used to tell me that. And you couldn't have been more right. All of us are simply puppets in the hands of God. He's putting on a great show. It really is quite magnificent. But if you have both feet planted squarely in the space-time continuum, there is no way you're going to understand it. People

208

like you are very rare. You know, as I do now, that *transcendence* is the only way out of the darkness. You have to get one foot beyond. Then you can endure this earthly life without disappointment and regret."

The old man's eyes twinkled as a yellow jacket buzzed past his nose. "As you use to tell me, every one of us has a part to play in God's special-effects drama. It's really true. A few of us have rather glamorous parts to play, but most of us are just blue-collar. We're all important, though. In God's eyes, we're all equal." The old man touched his hand to the warm blanket, feeling for its worldly texture. "In the end, though, we are all *sacrificed*. Some of us go early. Some of us last a long time. Some suffer terribly. Some cross over gently in their sleep. From where I stand, I see that nothing is really lost in the sacrifice. It's all just God playing around with His infinite potential. But from where the people stand in the world, it looks utterly brutal. That's why *transcendence* is so necessary. You have to get one foot beyond!"

Byron sat transfixed on the apparition before him. He stared at the old man's raincoat and felt a rush of levity. "What's with the London Fog? Are you chilly in the dead of summer? No pun intended."

The old man chuckled and unbuttoned his coat. As Byron leaned forward and looked into the void, the old man snickered. "Nobody's home."

Byron noticed a young couple weeping at a nearby gravesite. He looked at the old man with apprehension. The old man buttoned up his coat and raised himself to a standing position. It was as if he were floating on an invisible cloud. "No one else can see me, my friend. And no one else can hear me. As I said before, it is because of you that I can make contact. I only wear the coat and bring forth this old face for the convenience of that part of you that remains in the world."

The old man bowed to Byron with great respect and dignity. "You're doing good work here, my friend. You are a jewel in the rough."

Byron stood up, gently touched the old man's face, and felt the warmth of the summer air. "I have one question, Mark. Did Lisa Browning pass over without difficulty?"

The old man's face lit up with a wide smile. "Oh, yes. She is quite fine." Then his countenance evened out. "Here, there is no separation between beings. We all exist as one spirit. We're all quite fine." The old man glanced at the weeping couple nearby. "They weep for their own memories of the loved one. It brings no solace to the dead. No solace is necessary."

"It's human nature to grieve for the sacrificed," said Byron.

"Quite," said the old man.

Byron turned away in response to a piercing ambulance siren knifing through the soft summer breeze. When he turned back, the old man was gone.

61

They walked the wooded path along a dried-out riverbed about a mile east of Corbett Road. They advanced in silence as the shadows of summer twilight teased them with the coming darkness. Neither spoke for a good half-hour. Their mute progression was not the product of anger or avoidance or boredom. The silence had a deep energy to it. Dick Byron could feel the energy. It was engulfing them.

Linda Barnes stopped where the massive trunk of a fallen tree blocked their way. She hoisted herself up on the trunk and secured herself. "I'd like you to sit here with me," she said, patting the moist bark next to her. "I have something to tell you."

Byron slid up on the trunk next to her. He could feel his heart beating slowly beneath his breastbone. The dank smells of August and wood and moist soil and the nests of birds high above in the poplar trees filled his nostrils. He leaned back. His hands and forearms supported him on the trunk as his legs and feet elevated slightly.

"Something happened to me last week. I've been wanting to speak to you about it but haven't found the nerve until now." Barnes rubbed her nose self-consciously with the back of her hand. "I was working the night shift downtown. I got a call to break up a street fight on Guilford Avenue. A bunch of neighbors were arguing with a derelict—about who knows what—when the derelict pulled a gun on them. By the time I arrived, all of the neighbors had scattered. But sure enough, the derelict was there haunting the street, packing a very large .44 magnum."

Barnes shrugged her shoulders. "It was as if he had been waiting for me all along." She took a deep breath and continued. "At any rate, I drew my weapon, got out of my car, and began to approach him very cautiously. Then, all of a sudden, the son-of-a-bitch squared up and fired a wild shot over my head."

Barnes felt a strange tingling in her fingertips. She rubbed her hands together to avoid the distraction. "I'd never been shot at before. So needless to say, it didn't improve my mood. The next thing I knew, he was running like hell up Guilford Avenue. I chased him about a half-block until the son-of-a-bitch stopped, turned, and fired at me again. Another bullet whizzed over my head."

Barnes felt her stomach growl. *God, I'd love a stiff martini,* she thought. "Then I didn't know what was going on. I was madder than hell yet scared to death. The next thing I knew, I was chasing that bastard down the street. Eventually, I cornered him in a dead-end alley. I made him give up his gun, and I started to question him."

Barnes laughed knowingly. "When I look back on it, it was all too easy. But the way my life is going lately, nothing should surprise me."

Byron kicked the heels of his hiking boots together, and some dried clay fell to the ground. "Ah, an interesting comment. You're right. Nothing *should* surprise you. It's one bizarre universe we're participating in."

Barnes smiled and kicked Byron's right foot. *Thud!* "When you hear what I have to say, you'll think the universe is far stranger than you previously believed."

Byron nodded for her to go on.

Barnes felt her face flush with a mixture of embarrassment and anticipated happy disclosure. "I'm going to cut through all the bullshit and just lay out what happened." She felt a pull in her chest like an unruly tug-of-war. "The derelict was not human. He was some kind of angel or something. He knew all about me. About what I've been going through. He said he was there to help me." Barnes looked at Byron out of the corner of her eye. She couldn't look at him head on.

Byron nodded for her to continue.

Barnes shook her head. "I must be going fucking mad! The next thing I knew, he produced a white dove out of thin air. And the goddamn dove started talking to me." Her lips tightened in wary revelation. "The bottom line is this: The dove told me that help was already here. That I only needed to reach out and take its hand."

Barnes stared down at the ground in front of her. Out of the corner of her eye, she saw a hand appear. She took it in hers and squeezed tightly. Without looking at Byron, she declared, "You are the one, aren't you?"

"Yes. I'm the one." Byron took a deep breath. "I too know what you've been going through. If you allow me to help you, I will. But you have to *want* my help. You have to *surrender* to me."

Barnes closed her tired eyes. "The dark force within me is very strong. I no longer have much control over what I do."

"You have to *want* my help. You have to *surrender* to me."

Detective Linda Barnes. Tough-ass cop. She had no use for sentimentality, no use for small talk. She turned to Byron and shrugged her shoulders. She had nothing else to say.

Byron gently touched her face. "Muster up one last act of courage. If you sincerely *surrender* to me, I can help you. This is the only way it can work. As long as you perceive a personal will within you, the dark force has something to hang on to. But if you give up your personal life here and now, you become an instrument of God. God needs nothing to hang on to."

62

Tom Percy stared thoughtfully at the unobtrusive sign beside the doorway: **Brooklyn Zendo**. He glanced down at his stained, green, high-top Converse All-Star sneakers. An interesting contrast to the cleanly swept porch of the stately Victorian brownstone in Prospect Park, on the east edge of Brooklyn's Park Slope neighborhood.

Percy rang the doorbell and waited. He rang again and waited some more. He turned and stepped to the edge of the porch stairway. The bright sun hung high in the afternoon sky, and the warmth of its rays made the skin of his bare arms hum with an uncanny sensation of security. He hooked his thumbs in the corners of the front pockets of his blue jeans and gazed, with sweet leisure, at the pristine front yard. A single American elm reached its massive trunk majestically toward the heavens, while spreading its canopy of drooping branches and thick green leaves to grace the earthbound.

Percy's glance mysteriously gravitated to one of the lower branches of the American elm, where he saw perched a lone scarlet tanager. Its brilliant, scarlet red plumage blazed like fire around its shiny black wings and tail. *How odd*, thought Percy. *The scarlet tanager typically prefers the higher branches. It's as if this one is sacrificing its nature to get my attention.* Before Percy could complete his thought, the scarlet tanager took off in flight—up one side of the elm's leafy canopy and down the other, finally coming to light on the sidewalk a few yards before the brownstone's stairway. The majestic bird pointed its beak upward and moved its head systematically, as if surveying the upper reaches of the house.

Tom Percy tiptoed lightly down the stairway. He turned and looked up at the old brownstone. He could see lacy curtains moving gently in the breeze behind raised windows on the second and third floors. Percy contemplatively rubbed his stubble-bearded chin and looked down at the bird as it chirped sweetly and took flight around the side of the house.

Percy followed the avian lead and when he turned the corner, found his winged friend perched on an elderberry bush. As Percy approached, the fiery black tanager danced to an adjacent sweet pepper bush and finally disappeared around the back of the house.

Tom Percy laughed to himself as he playfully chased after the bird. The leisure in his gait was new to him. Ever since he had decided to leave journalism behind, everything seemed new to him.

The backyard of the brownstone was surrounded by a freshly painted redwood picket fence. For some reason, Percy had no feelings of trespassing. Lifting the silver-colored hook of the fence gate was as natural to him as breathing. He felt that he belonged there. When he closed the gate behind him and latched the hook, he felt an odd sense of loss—not at all disagreeable. It was as if his past happily disintegrated behind him.

The contents of the backyard rushed him in segments. First, he saw the scarlet tanager. It had alighted on the edge of an old stone birdbath and was picking at some water with its beak. The birdbath was covered with soft, green moss and looked like a cool haven for something wanting to escape a terrible heat. The tanager wasn't escaping anything, however. It was just drinking the cool water as if it had been planned that way long ago.

Then he saw the man. A thin, wiry, olive-complexioned man sitting on the stone patio next to the birdbath. The man wore a black T-shirt and khakis and was barefooted. His shaven head was bent forward, and his left knee was tucked up under his chin. Both hands were engaged with his left foot. *For God's sake,* mused Percy, *he's trimming his toenails.*

Suddenly the man looked up. His eyes slanted pleasantly along the contours of his long, chiseled, Asian face. A massive smile spread across his countenance as naturally as water seeks its common level. "Welcome, my friend. Welcome. I'm so happy to see you!"

Tom Percy laughed self-consciously. "I don't mean to interrupt you. I tried ringing the bell out front, but no one answered."

The Asian, continuing to smile, clipped at another toenail and rubbed his fingers gently across the tips of his toes. He carefully closed the nail clipper and placed it in a small, leather bag lying next to him on the patio. Then he took a deep breath and effortlessly raised himself to a standing position. "My name is Maha Ananda. I am the Zen master here at the Brooklyn Zendo."

Percy bowed to the master with deep respect. *At last, I'm where I'm supposed to be,* he thought. "My name is Tom Percy. You are the person I have come to see. I want to become a Zen Buddhist."

Maha Ananda smiled with compassion. "Are you sure this is what you want?"

"Yes. I'm positive."

"Be careful, my friend. You may not like being a Zen Buddhist." Maha Ananda's eyes reflected a happy balance between serious caution and humorous abandonment. "Many people think a Zen Buddhist is always floating in the sky, soaring happily above the clouds. I'm here to warn you that this is not the case."

Percy smiled. His lungs filled with an intoxicating purity that was completely novel. "I know what I'm getting into. I simply want your blessing and your guidance. Will you be my teacher?"

Maha Ananda took a deep breath. He had been at this crossroad so many times before. The caretaking of a soul was no small matter.

"Let's have a cup of tea together and talk. This is not something you want to rush into."

Tom nodded. "Okay. That sounds reasonable."

63

Maha Ananda poured piping hot Numi Golden Chai tea into two gold-rimmed Carolina blue china teacups. The thick aroma of the tea filled the small kitchen with a mystical, fragrant blend of cinnamon, ginger, cardamom, and anise. The kitchen was very simple and orderly. All necessary things in their places. Nothing left over.

The Zen master, holding his cup in both hands, closed his eyes and sipped the tea with great concentration. "Ah," he said. "It is the nectar of the gods." Maha Ananda stared at his guest from somewhere beyond space and time. "Okay. Tell me why you want to be a Zen Buddhist."

Tom Percy cautiously sipped his tea. It was *damn* hot. The tea burned his lips but not unpleasantly. It made him feel alive and aware. "A week ago, I left my job at the *Village Voice*. I've been a writer for the past twenty years." Percy shrugged his shoulders, and a wry smile spread across his face. "I was going along just fine until a year ago, when I traveled to India to do a story on a mysterious guru by the name of Sri Peche." Percy found the warm teacup in his hands to be pleasantly soothing. "Do you know him?"

Maha Ananda blinked his eyes slowly, meditatively. "No. I don't know him."

Percy took a sip of tea. It had cooled a bit, and the flavors had melded softly like the right combination of grapes in a fine French wine. "Needless to say, he is quite something. I was with him for about a week. The man who said hello to him was not the man who said good-bye."

Maha Ananda smiled knowingly. "Sometimes it happens that way."

Percy rubbed his fingers across his chin. The stubble reminded him that he could use a shave. "Sri Peche made me realize that I needed to take my life in a different direction. He made me realize the value of serving humanity without asking for anything in return."

Percy looked at the Zen master, awaiting some kind of response. Maha Ananda radiated a cool stillness that was completely receptive. No response was necessary. Tom Percy continued. "That's why I've come to you. That's why I want to be a Zen Buddhist."

Maha Ananda quizzically cocked his head. "Why don't you go to Sri Peche? It sounds as if he could give you what you want."

Percy stared into his teacup. Black tea swirling in upon itself. No beginning, no end. "I wrote to him recently. I told him I wanted to come back to India. I told him I wanted to be with him." Percy leaned back in his chair. He felt centered and relaxed. He smiled and chuckled. "He told me that I should find a good Zen master in New York. He said that Zen was the most direct path to realization. He said he wanted me serving in the trenches of humanity. He said being a recluse in India lacked courage."

Maha Ananda sat straight up in his chair. "Sri Peche is an interesting character. How does he know so much about Zen Buddhism?"

"I don't know," said Percy. "But I trust him."

Maha Ananda shook his head and smiled. "So be it."

Tom Percy felt his body go strangely numb as Maha Ananda leaned in closely and whispered, "Mr. Percy, excuse my language, but this is *very serious shit*. I have one question to ask you, and I want you to consider it very carefully."

Percy, feeling curiously hypnotized, heard himself say, "Go ahead, ask your question."

Maha Ananda's eyes blazed like fire. Very slowly and distinctly, he said, "Are you ready to *suffer*?"

Percy winced. "What?"

"Are you ready to *suffer*?"

Percy felt the blood drain from his head, and a faint pain welled up behind his eyeballs. "I don't know. To be honest, I think I'd rather *avoid* suffering, if that's possible."

Maha Ananda smiled and nodded gracefully. "A very honest answer. I like that." A rush of deafening silence surged through the kitchen like a negative sonic blast from a jet plane. Ear-piercing yet completely silent. "I ask this question because Zen Buddhism is about complete and utter fearlessness. This nonsense of worrying about your own pleasure and security is a thing of the past. If you are not ready to completely pass through your own suffering, you cannot live as a Zen Buddhist."

Tom Percy sat in utter shock in the kitchen in Prospect Park with the Chai tea and the Zen master. He tried to speak, but no words came forth. But then, as if someone were speaking for him, he heard himself say, "Tell me what I must do. I'm at the end of my rope. I cannot live this way any longer."

Maha Ananda leaned back in his chair. He smiled and bowed his head. Then he looked up and bore a deep stare into Percy's soul. "All right. I will be your master. This is not a one-way street, however. In a way, it is a marriage. You completely devote yourself to me and the teachings of Zen Buddhism, and I completely devote myself to you as your unfailing guide. We can *never ever* give up on each other. Do you understand?"

Tom Percy took a long, deep breath. "I understand completely."

Maha Ananda nodded and sipped his tea with circumspection. "In Zen Buddhism, we drop our body and mind in the incinerator and devote all of our waking energy to relieving the suffering of others. We cannot stop the suffering, but we can relieve it. We no longer care about our own comfort or our own dignity. We do whatever needs to be done to help others who are suffering."

Tom cocked his head and concentrated his eyes as if he were a dog desperately trying to understand what his beloved master was saying.

Maha Ananda's eyes expressed a deep patience. "Are you ready to help others? Will you make that commitment?"

Tom Percy, feeling stronger by the minute, leaned forward. "Yes, I am ready to make the commitment."

"Okay, then. Let me tell you what needs to be done." Maha Ananda gracefully rubbed his forehead, as if to clear away any residue of mental condensation. "Sri Peche is correct. Zen Buddhism does not put up with any bullshit. The path is direct and clear. It involves two essential ingredients: wisdom and compassion. That is all. Both are within you already. They simply need to be unearthed and allowed to breathe. Both wisdom and compassion will surface from the disciplines of meditation, non-attachment, and fearlessness. I will guide you in all of these disciplines. But I must warn you here and now: Wisdom and compassion are *not* what you think they are. They are far beyond your rational reckonings."

Tom Percy felt himself leaning forward with great concentration. Simply listening to the words of Maha Ananda energized him. "I'll do whatever you say. I am in your hands."

"One more thing, my dear friend. I am not going to be easy on you.

221

You will suffer at my hands. I'm going to reduce your ego to ashes. There is no other way. You will have to have complete faith in me, even as I cook your mind and body to ashes."

Tom Percy looked at Maha Ananda through determined eyes. "I don't care anymore. Do what you will with me. I trust you."

Maha Ananda raised himself from his chair and stood before his new devotee. "In Zen Buddhism, we make a very clear distinction between *true* compassion and *idiot* compassion. Do you know what the difference is?"

Percy looked up into the eyes of his master. His heart skipped a beat when he realized that no human being existed behind those eyes. The whole universe, in its entirety, undulated there like some vast infinite ocean. "No, I do not."

Maha Ananda smiled. "Good. It is good *not* to know. When we *think* we know something, we get into trouble. It is better *not* to know. In this way, the mind always remains open and receptive to what's coming next."

Percy smiled. He could feel his mind aching for wisdom. "Well, I should be a good student. I feel at a complete loss right now."

Maha Ananda seemed oblivious to Percy's remark. "Idiot compassion takes place when we feel *sorry* for someone. When we feel they cannot handle the truth, we make excuses to lie to them so they won't feel any worse than they already do. This is not so good."

Maha Ananda looked up at the kitchen ceiling, as if in search of the perfect words of explanation. The ceiling fan, whirling above, hummed what sounded like an ancient hymn of peaceful condolence. "Idiot compassion is syrupy and sticky. It does no good to anyone. True compassion, on the other hand, genuinely heals the wounds of suffering. Sometimes the wounds need to be cleaned. It can be unpleasant, but it is necessary for the healing to take place. As a Zen Buddhist, you cannot be afraid to clean the wounds of suffering. You cannot be afraid to do work that soils your hands. You must be willing to live in the trenches."

Tom Percy stared at his master with wonder. "With your guidance, I'm sure I'll be up to the task."

Maha Ananda nodded respectfully. "We shall see." The Zen master gently lifted his teacup from the table and carefully placed it in the sink. "More tea, Mr. Percy?"

"No, I'm fine. Thank you."

Maha Ananda opened a drawer adjacent to the sink, pulled out a bright yellow apron, slipped it over his head, and efficiently tied the apron cords around his waist. The yellow apron was emblazoned with a giant red turtle and the words *Maryland Terrapins.*

Tom Percy shook his head and giggled. *This is so funny*, he thought. "Are you a Terps fan?"

Maha Ananda looked down at the apron and smiled proudly. "Oh, yes. I like the Terps. I like Gary Williams. He coaches with such fire and intensity." The Zen master winked with resolve. "He has *no* idiot compassion."

Tom Percy broke into a wide smile. He felt the skin around the outside corners of his eyes crinkle pleasantly. A surging happiness filled his heart.

Maha Ananda carefully cleaned his teacup with a soapy, wet dishcloth and dried it, methodically, with a hand towel. Then he carefully placed the cup in the cupboard above the sink. "May I clean your cup, Mr. Percy?"

Tom Percy drained his cup with one last, quick sip and respectfully passed the cup to his master. "Thank you for the tea. It was delightful."

"You're very welcome, Mr. Percy." Maha Ananda cleaned Tom's cup with the same careful intentionality and placed it in the cupboard. "A Zen Buddhist tries to do whatever he is doing with utter perfection. Even cleaning teacups." Maha Ananda's smile filled the room with light and lightness. "You see, cleaning the cups is part of the enjoyment of drinking the tea. We believe that the drinking is not over until we have cleaned the cups. And it is so nice to have clean cups waiting for you the next time you invite a guest to drink tea."

Tom Percy gazed at his master with great appreciation. Maha Ananda removed his apron, folded it carefully, and returned it to the drawer next to the sink. He playfully leaned back on his heels. "So do you have any other questions for me?"

Tom Percy smiled and shrugged his shoulders with happy resolve.

"Okay. That's good. I'll walk you to the front porch."

Tom Percy walked with his master through a small, simply furnished dining room and living room. No pictures or statues of the Buddha. No incense. Nothing left over. Just the sweet resonance of order and peace.

When Maha Ananda opened the front screen door, there was the slightest squeak, nearly imperceptible. "Ah, did you hear that? When you leave, I'll get the WD-40." Maha Ananda seemed pleased to have heard the squeak. He seemed pleased at the prospect of fixing the door.

Tom Percy stood on the front porch of the Prospect Park brownstone with a lightness in his heart he had rarely, if ever, experienced. It made him think of resting in the arms of a sweet lover, knowing that he will be back in her arms again very soon. "Maha Ananda. May I come see you again tomorrow?"

Maha Ananda smiled and gently held his hands together in front of him at his waist. "I want to see you in one week." A pregnant pause filled the afternoon's open stillness. "I want you to be *very thirsty* when you come back."

Tom Percy shook his head and smiled meekly. He could feel a sense of loss welling up within him. He didn't know what to say. Finally, he said spontaneously, "Do you know that you are *very* unpredictable?"

Maha Ananda smiled proudly. "Oh, thank you so much. Yes, unpredictable. That's me."

64

Tom Percy sorted through his mail at the dining room table with nagging distraction. He was still riding high after his meeting with the Zen master and simply could not stop thinking about Maha Ananda and the long week that lay ahead. He so much wanted to be in his master's presence. *Ah, hell,* he thought. *He said I would suffer. I guess I'll just have to get used to this.*

Out of the washed-out whiteness of the pile of envelopes, one mysteriously demanded his attention. It was postmarked from India. It was from Sri Peche.

Dear Mr. Percy:

I hope this note finds you well and in good spirits.

If God were to create the cosmos and put all the forces of nature into motion, and then sit back and hold us **responsible** *for all that happens, it would be the cruelest of tricks. Our life would be a nightmare of suffering and ignorance from which we could never wake.*

If God were to create the cosmos and put all the forces of nature into motion, and then sit back and witness the drama of his own making through the eyes of his creations, holding no one responsible but Himself, it would be the most wonderful of special-effects productions. If we were to fully realize this, our life would be one of duty and service to God. We would selflessly act out our part in the drama as God has willed it and would no longer be plagued with questions or burdened with doubts.

Surrender. Acceptance. Service. Peace.

(Just between the two of us, I think Shakespeare was a very special incarnation of God.)

Bless you.

Sri Peche

65

One Year Later

He sat at a table on the second-story terrace of a bar overlooking the Place Djemaa el-Fna in Marrakech. One-half hour before, a heavy downpour had raged through the city, leaving the stone surface of the bazaar square and the tiny alleys emanating from it wet and steamy.

The lights had just come on. Streetlamps, shop lamps, the rainbow colors of tiny ornamental lights, strung together, outlining the shops and rooflines of the bazaar. A kaleidoscopic scene of light and reflections of light, mixing in congress with the movements of men, women, and children in brightly colored robes; mist rising off the hot, damp streets; the smells of incense and fruit and vegetables and meat and burning oil; the sounds of drums and horns and flutes and the hum of incessant chatter and bartering.

Two empty wineglasses sat on the table before him. He flagged down a waiter and ordered another. An hour passed. He paid the bill, descended onto the street, and merged with the magic bustle of the bazaar. Stopping to watch a snake charmer, he felt someone brush by him a little too intimately. A beautiful, young girl eyed him over her shoulder as she disappeared into the crowd. A seminal urge rose in his loins, and a guttural growl came up from the bottom of his belly. As if he were a wolf smelling blood, he dashed off in pursuit of the girl.

The game of hide-and-seek moved erratically through the maze of glistening alleyways, past the multitude of shops selling rugs and dyes and spices and tapestries. At each corner, he caught a glimpse of her—and then she was gone—and then she was there again. Finally, the hunt terminated at a butcher shop at the far end of an alley. The girl hovered in the doorway of the shop. Giant animal carcasses hung all around her like macabre ornaments of horror. She allowed him to see her and then retreated inside.

He approached the shop entrance with graceful caution—like a wild animal seeking its prey. At times like this, he was no longer human. Some force within him, something burning and alien, took over. He liked the feeling of raw brutality. It was transcendental. He moved through the shop door, pushing the animal carcasses to the side. There, he encountered a souk trader. The trader smiled widely. No teeth in this mouth—just blood red gums and a pale tongue. A crooked finger pointed excitedly to a rickety stairway leading to the second floor.

He maneuvered up the stairway, two steps at a time, as if he were a genetic mishap resulting in some grotesque human-canine hybrid. He entered a shadow-laden room at the top of the stairway. The room was illuminated by a single candle burning on a small table next to a series of worn mattresses piled upon one another.

The girl smiled and caressed her breasts through her blouse. "Fifteen dollars, mister. Fifteen dollars, you get this."

He stood in a still crouch. Looking at her intently. Breathing steadily. He felt his lips stretch back over his teeth as he smiled. He growled, *"I don't think so, sweetie."*

The girl was no longer smiling. The red-black eyes of the beast before her crushed her fortitude. And then he was on her. From downstairs, the souk trader heard a single, ravenous cry and a cascade of hideous wailing. He grabbed his wooden staff and approached the stairway but then stopped, frozen in terror. The sounds coming from the top of the stairway were not of this world. They were something from the lower regions of hell. The trader crumpled to the floor in a state of catatonia and regained consciousness only after some time. There was nothing but silence. The kind of silence signifying that everything familiar has ended, that nothing will ever be the same.

66

Chelsea–Thornton Peachwater lifted the receiver from its cradle. "Hello."

"Hi, dear. How are you?"

"Oh, Elliot. It's so good to hear from you. How did the conference go?"

"Well, you know how these conferences are. A bit tedious. I thought my presentation went well. But, of course, they always do."

"That's great, Elliot. They're lucky to have you."

"Yes, I suppose you're right," Peachwater said, smiling to himself with earnest satisfaction. "At any rate, I'm off to the airport and should be home late tonight."

"Wonderful, Elliot. I can't wait to see you. I love you."

"Bye, dear. Love you, too." Peachwater hung up the phone. *Oh, what a silly, silly cow,* he thought.

Elliot Peachwater walked into the bathroom and pulled a plastic bag out of the tub. His bloodstained clothes were visible through the clear plastic. He took the bag, wrapped it securely in newspaper, and inserted the whole bundle into an opaque dark green plastic garbage bag. He heard the maid vacuuming in the hallway. *Right on time,* he thought. He carried the bag into the hallway. The maid, dressed in her pressed, white uniform, turned off her vacuum cleaner and faced Peachwater.

"Good morning," Peachwater said. "Would you be so kind as to throw this away for me?"

67

Six Months Later

Dick Byron stared out the window of his study. A compact tape recorder, into which he was dictating ideas for an article on Dietrich Bonhoeffer, sat on a small table behind his desk. As Byron paused to collect his thoughts, a flock of geese flew across the gray sky, honking a mysterious melody of resolve.

It was cold this early December morning, and the cup of hot coffee he held in his hands comforted him, if only for a moment. Byron loved the still, quiet mornings on this Monkton hillside, but today the quiet was eerie and foreboding. Something was coming.

Standing in the kitchen, pouring his second cup of coffee, he heard the crisp *ping* of the doorbell. When he opened the door and saw who it was, his heart skipped a beat. Elliot Peachwater stood before him.

Both men silently eyed each other.

"Well, if it isn't my favorite priest," Peachwater said. "Are you going to invite me in?"

Byron said nothing as he moved aside and motioned, with a sweep of his hand, for Peachwater to enter. Peachwater immediately encountered the life-size statue of St. Francis. "My God, Byron, I always knew you took this man seriously; but to cohabitate with him is a bit much, wouldn't you say?"

"To tell you the truth, Elliot, he's very little trouble. Pretty much keeps to himself."

"Yes, those renunciates can be pretty standoffish."

Byron had enough of the pseudointellectual bantering. "Well, Elliot, what brings you here?"

"Ah, a good question, Father Dick. But before we get down to the serious matters of life, could I trouble you for a cup of coffee? Yours smells quite heavenly."

Byron showed Peachwater to the study. After courteously relieving his visitor of his dark gray herringbone Chesterfield overcoat and fire engine red Burberry scarf, which he carefully placed over the seat of one of two Queen Anne chairs adjacent to the coffee table, Byron retreated to the kitchen for another cup of coffee. When he returned, he found Peachwater casually eyeing the books in his library.

"I see you're still reading this mystical rubbish. One would think you would have graduated to the real world by now," said Peachwater.

Byron handed the coffee to Peachwater and sat down behind his desk. Peachwater situated himself comfortably in the vacant Queen Anne chair. As he was doing so, Byron deftly placed his hand on the tape recorder and pushed the RECORD button.

"Well, Elliot, what can I do for you?"

"Well, Dick, the truth is I've been thinking about you lately. Does that surprise you?"

"Where you're concerned, Elliot, nothing surprises me."

"Ah, I see. Well, let me get straight to the point. I have a confession to make, and seeing that you're a Catholic priest who takes his duties *very* seriously, I know that everything I say will remain in strict confidence."

Byron said nothing.

"Do you understand, Dick? I'm making a formal confession. I'm asking for absolution."

"Go on," Byron said calmly.

Peachwater tipped his head back slightly, and the eerie little laugh that came from his lips spoke of insanity. "Well, Dick, I don't think you've ever heard a confession like this one before. In fact, it's especially for you. Only someone holier-than-thou could bear this cross."

Byron, saying nothing, kept his eyes glued to Peachwater's.

"As you know, Dick, I've never liked you. In fact, I've always found you to be an insufferable bore. You and all your spirituality. Well, my friend, I'm going to give you a story that you can take to your grave. Remember, no cheating. This is a confession. You're bound by your vows not to go to the coppers."

Byron said nothing.

"Dick, as you well know, I've always had a thing for the ladies. And, I must admit, they have reciprocated quite nicely. Some time ago, however, one of the cute little bitches did something very stupid. You know what she did? She got pregnant. Can you believe it? Even after I explained to her the delicacies of my position on abortion, she would have none of it." Peachwater smiled sardonically. "Well, to make a long story short, I relieved her of all her troubles."

Byron thoughtfully sipped his coffee. Out of the corner of his eye, he could see the tape slowly turning in the recorder. "What do you mean when you say you relieved her of all her troubles?"

Peachwater smiled a sickening smile, his face turning red. "I killed her."

Byron spoke very deliberately. "What was her name?"

"What?"

"What was her name? If I'm to pray for her soul, I need to know her name."

"Her name, oh, holy Father, was Hillary Miles."

Byron stared at Peachwater but said nothing.

Peachwater took a deep, exasperated breath, as if the conversation were unbearably tedious. "And that's not all. No, my dear spiritual friend, there's more for you to bear with Jesus. As it turned out, Ms. Miles had a big mouth and told someone else about the bastard growing inside her. So there I was. More work for weary, old Elliot. Do you want her name, as well, for your saving prayers?"

"Yes."

"Lisa Browning. I believe you knew her." Peachwater smiled, his eyes twinkling mischievously. "An unusual woman. Seemed she was prepared to commit suicide. I just helped her along."

"Helped her along?"

"For your God's sake, Byron, yes," Peachwater said with an arrogant flash of irritation at having to lead the witless. "Helped her along. Killed her too. Flouted the fifth commandment yet again."

Byron was surprised by his own centeredness and perspicacity. He felt himself curiously floating above the scene as if he were a disinterested witness. "Why are you telling me this, Elliot?"

"Because, Father Byron, I don't like you. I don't like your

condescending spiritual claptrap. I just thought I'd give you a little cross to bear. After all, Dick, that's what you saints are here for—to help the rest of us pitiful creatures who don't know any better."

Byron cocked his head quizzically. "Why did you wait so long to bring me this news?"

Peachwater broke out into a hyena-like laugh. "Well, I do have a rather busy schedule. The stories I could tell you. But they can wait for another time." Peachwater's eyes turned a glossy gray. Hardly human. "Let's just say you had to wait your turn."

Saying nothing, Byron continued to eye Peachwater.

"Well, Dickie, how many *Hail Marys* am I condemned to? What would you say these little transgressions are worth?"

Byron said nothing.

The two men sat, eye to eye, in deafening silence. Finally, Peachwater placed his empty cup on the coffee table next to him. He feigned a pained grimace. "Well, Dick, does God forgive me?"

"I wouldn't know," Byron said, looking into the face of pure oblivion before him.

Peachwater leaned back in his chair and ran both of his hands slowly through his thick, gray hair. "Well, I must admit I'm disappointed. I came all this way for nothing," he intoned with mock disgust.

Peachwater stood up and shook his head dismissively. He put on his overcoat and scarf and made his way to leave the room. When he reached the doorway, Peachwater turned and looked at his confessor, who was still sitting behind the desk. Byron could see the man framed in the doorway very clearly. The colors of his hair, eyes, skin, and clothes were surrealistically bright and sharp—and then, everything faded to gray. Peachwater started to speak—and then, his face contorted into a mask of sudden, inert horror. Byron watched as the form before him began to melt, to dissolve, as if in some monstrous furnace—and then, there was nothing.

Byron sat in his chair behind the desk in his study for an indeterminate length of time. It was long after he had heard Peachwater drive away in his car; long after he had heard the moving about in adjacent rooms and the running of the shower.

"Dick...Dick, are you okay?"

Dick looked up. "Yes. I'm fine."

"You look like you've seen a ghost."

"I think I have."

The woman came around behind the desk and sat on Dick's lap, putting her left arm around his neck. She moved her fingers gently through his hair. "What's happened, honey?" she said coyly and then added a phrase that had become second nature to them: "You can tell me. I'm a homicide cop who's here to protect you."

68

One Year Later

The Clifton T. Perkins Hospital. Jessup, Maryland. Maximum-Security Forensic Psychiatric Ward. A man in gray overalls sits at a wooden desk. The colorless walls surrounding him are concrete. The floor is made of tattered, brown linoleum. In one corner sits a cot with worn mattress and yellowed sheets. Across the room is a toilet and washbasin. Two fluorescent lights flicker above.

The man has long, unkempt, gray hair. The hair has a wild, electrical fuzziness about it. Perhaps a physical extension of the electrical psychic storm inside his skull. A bushy, gray beard covers his face. The eyes peering out above the beard are cunning and cold. Pale, icy blue in color. The tops of his ears protrude through the fuzzy, gray hair. *Pointy. Reddish. Odd.*

The man is concentrating on something. Intently. A fly. Perched on the desk. The fly has red eyes. Soft, translucent wings. In a flicker of light, a hand *flashes out* and seizes its prey. The fist, closing gently. A tickling buzz against the palm. Now, slowly to the mouth. The head tilts back. The eyes close with satisfaction. In through the lips. A faint buzzing between the cheek and gum. *Crunch...crunch.* And swallow.

Down the hall, not fifty feet from the fly-eater, is a waiting room. A woman sits there alone, reading a book. She is elderly and very well dressed. Her name is Olivia Brownstone.

A burly orderly, dressed in white, enters the waiting room. "Ms. Brownstone, I don't think your son is ready for you today. He's not feeling well. Perhaps you could come back later in the week."

Ms. Brownstone looks up from her book. *Saint Genet. Jean-Paul*

Sartre. "No, I think not. I'm here now and will see him. I'm not squeamish."

The orderly scratches his head. "I don't mean to be difficult. But I really don't think it's in your best interest to see him today."

Ms. Brownstone raises herself from the chair. She is tall and thin. There is something menacing about her. She looks at the nametag pinned to the orderly's shirt pocket. "Mr. Toomy, I don't mean to be difficult either. I want to see my son. Seeing him in a bad state will not alarm me. Believe me, I've seen things in my life much worse than an insane man in his meager quarters."

Ms. Brownstone takes two steps forward and is nose-to-nose with Toomy. She locks her eyes on his. Rocks her head slowly from side to side, looking deep into his eyes, feeling her way into his cranium. Smiling now. Pointy teeth glistening on her lower lip.

She has what she wants.

Toomy suddenly rocks back on his heels, his hands cupped to his eyes. *The pain is unbearable.* He drops to his knees. His hands fall from his eyes. Blood-stained hands. Blood-stained cheeks. Toomy collapses to the floor as if in slow motion and regresses into the fetal position.

Ms. Olivia Brownstone is now twenty feet down the hall, walking gracefully. A light bounce in her step. Only thirty feet to Sonny-boy.

The fly-eater licks his lips and cocks his head upward. *Someone's coming.* His eyes roll back beneath his brow. *Mommy.*

Ms. Brownstone peers through the tiny, green-tinted glass window on the cell door. She sees him now. She rolls her eyes back beneath her brow. *My dear, dear Elliot. Mommy is here.*

The fly-eater smiles. *I know. It's wonderful to hear your voice.* He sees another fly. *I'm eating quite well today. The oppressive heating system in this hellhole encourages the flies to hatch. Lucky for me, they somehow find their way in here.*

Elliot, I'm a bit pressed for time. Your friend Mr. Toomy has come to an unfortunate impasse. I can't hang around to see how it turns out.

Another fly is being stalked. *I understand, Mom. We're all so busy these days.*

Elliot, I just wanted to know: would you like me to pay a visit to Mr. Byron? I could do something nasty to him. After all, he is responsible for your unfortunate situation.

A fly buzzes softly within the fly-eater's closed fist. *It makes me laugh to hear you say* **Mister** *Byron. Ah, how the worm turns.* He takes a deep, satisfying breath. *I think we'll just leave well enough alone. That cute little copper-girlfriend will be enough of a disappointment to him.* A shrill, spine-tingling giggle comes up from his belly. *Did you know there is a bit of us in her? Oh, yes. It was somewhat latent for a while but sure to be manifesting in full bloom by now. I think she was waiting for the good father.*

Ms. Brownstone shivers pleasantly at the thought. *Oh, how delicious. Sweetie, I'm off.*

On the parking lot outside Clifton T. Perkins, a strong gust of wind blows Ms. Brownstone's hair up and away from her ears. *Pointy. Reddish. Odd.*

Printed in the United States
79502LV00002B/547-570